GHOSTS IN THE VALLEY

GHOSTS IN THE VALLEY
& other stories

RICHARD STEELE

STEELE ROBERTS
AOTEAROA NEW ZEALAND

'Forgotten World Highway 43' – photo by Helmut Hirler.
www.helmut-hirler.de/html/neuseeland_0.html

National Library of New Zealand Cataloguing-in-Publication Data
Steele, Richard, 1948-
Ghosts in the Valley & other stories / Richard Steele.
ISBN 978-1-877448-32-4
1. Short stories, New Zealand. 2. New Zealand fiction—
21st century. I. Title.
NZ823.3 —dc 22

The story 'Ghosts in the Valley' is a work of fiction, and any resemblance to real persons, living or dead, is purely coincidental.

Royalties from this book go to the
Rural Support Trust, supporting isolated rural families.

Thanks to Anna, Colin, Helen, Jan, Les, Lyndal, Michèle and Rachel for typing, editing and proofreading; to Helmut Hirler for the cover photo, and Luk Chin for the author photo. Set in 10.5pt Baskerville and printed by Publishing Press, Auckland.

STEELE ROBERTS PUBLISHERS
Box 9321 Wellington Aotearoa New Zealand
info@SteeleRoberts.co.nz • www.SteeleRoberts.co.nz

Contents

Ghosts in the Valley

I

At twenty past four I decided to turn around and go home. Liz and I had been walking for about five hours, and while she could walk like this all day, I was worn out. A year ago I'd sliced through my right calf in a wood-chopping mishap and though the wound had healed well, long-distance walking was still a bit of an effort.

Liz is a bitch, a heading dog, a pleasure to walk with. She often saw things I didn't notice, certainly smelt things I didn't smell and sometimes picked up movement long before I did.

We were searching for missing cows. Six weeks earlier I had put 150 cows into the Teapot Valley to winter over until calving — cleaning up rank grass which the sheep had left all summer, and mooching around in scrubby regrowth. Four days ago, in a fairly thorough coverage of all the open country, the boys had mustered out 140 and found only two dead. We suspected the remaining eight had wandered into the neighbouring National Park.

At around half past ten that morning I had parked my ATV, my all-terrain vehicle, on the main Kaiwhakauku track. Turning east from the track I had climbed up through the Teapot Valley to the saddle between Teapot and Sammie's back gully. From this vantage point on a good clear day like today you could see a fair number of the grassy patches amongst the regrown scrub, and pick out cattle that had wandered into the open areas to feed or warm up in the winter sun.

Heading south from the saddle, then west along Sammie's back gully, we had seen four of them. Two out in the clearings from the tops and two Liz had pointed at like a gun dog. Cows standing quietly in the scrub as we walked past. This was where Liz earned her dinner. Often, where I was busy concentrating on the rutted track in front of me, she would stop and stare. Sometimes with one front foot raised, head pointing directly towards whatever she had sensed. As soon as I noticed her it was only a moment before I had worked out what was there. Often it was a possum up a tree, very occasionally a pig. Pigs and possums made her hackles rise. In this case it was cows, standing quietly. Cows just got the stare.

Once we got back onto the Kaiwhakauku track, rather than walk north back to the vehicle, I looked at my watch, did a quick appraisal of my leg and turned south through Spratts' and Hamers' — blocks named after original settlers — towards the National Park. From this part of the track we could look into clearings on the open faces for cattle that had pushed south.

After about half an hour we came to the park boundary, fenced off from our grazing land with a narrow locked gate for Department of Conservation staff, and a stile provided for trampers. I hauled myself over the stile while Liz pushed through the wires and we continued south for a long while, another hour at least, so I could be sure as possible that cows had not escaped around or through the fence somewhere and grazed south. No signs, no tracks, no cows. Just a walk.

These old abandoned roads are far gentler to wander along than our own rugged farm tracks, in terms of gradient at least. They were put in nearly a century ago for people walking into their blocks and for horses bearing loads or pulling carts, so they never went up or down at more than three degrees.

Our own tracks and fencelines were carved out by bulldozers and diggers and traversed largely on foot, horseback or 4 x 4 ATVs in the last decade or so. Grade or steepness of the land is not such a problem as it was to the first settlers here around the time of the First World War.

The track followed the Kaiwhakauku Stream, engraved deep into the papa rock and surrounded by regenerating native bush. It was a perfect habitat of the rare whio, a whistling duck not often seen. Today I saw neither ducks nor cows, but just enjoyed the stroll.

This is hard-case country to farm, compared to a square farm on the flats with all the buildings centrally located, with a race system for stock movement.

Our land tends to follow valleys running north and south from our home base, utilising the more fertile river flats and easier hills facing north, but ignoring steep southern faces or ridges leading to bluffs. Overall the farm is about 18 kilometres long and follows the tracks, but there's often some distance between patches of productive pasture.

This spread-out terrain means a number of things to a farmer. Every day is an adventure at best, or an enjoyable ride around at least. When you leave the house in the morning intending to do an hour's work moving the ewes or whatever, sometimes you're home in an hour, sometimes eight. This means you have to let people know where you are — which is just about where I am up to now.

I'd left home Sunday morning around ten to have a quiet look for a few missing cows. I had gone further than I intended to go, taken more side gullies, probably walked more slowly. Soon, if I wasn't careful, someone would be starting to wonder where the hell I was. And then start looking, which would be a waste of everyone's time as I was quite okay. But you never know.

On our farm it's a policy that if someone's overdue, go looking … now. It will most likely be a wasted trip, but far better a wasted trip in the daylight than searching at night when everything is trickier. Last year, Murray and I had gone out late in the evening looking for a neighbour's son who had gone out pig hunting for a couple of hours in the morning and well overdue. Even trying to find his ATV tracks at night was slow; finding the boy himself took until the following day. An easy lesson learnt. He was fine, and in daylight his ATV stood out for miles.

So here I was at half-past four on the way home to our old bungalow above the Whanganui River, 60 kilometres from the nearest town, Taumarunui. Actually three houses, shearers' quarters, a woolshed and a toolshed in a hectare of garden. This is trees, mainly, six of which have been there for 90 years, including a huge copper beech and an impressive oak. We have lived here for twenty years.

In the old house there's me — Tony Price — and my wife of 30 years, Georgina. House number two also overlooks the river; it's a Lockwood where younger son Campbell lives with his partner Julia, who works as a canoeing guide on the Whanganui. Number three is where my son Jack lives, so far on his own, waiting for his family to catch up. Jack's married to Andrea, who will be here with their son and daughter — our first grandchildren — when their house in Whakatane is sold. We built house number three ourselves and are quite proud of the modest achievement that it at least doesn't leak.

Murray has been the only permanent resident in the shearers' quarters. He's in his early twenties and works for us as a shepherd, but he's buggering off soon to study agriculture at Lincoln. He will be definitely missed.

Liz and I ambled along, heading north with the rippling water on our right. I realised, not for the first time, how the water here coming down from the abandoned old farms in the National Park is noticeably cleaner. Darker with bush leachate after rain, but cleaner than farm run-off, and hence most of its beauty as it swirls over the rocks and reflects the colours of the bush. Must plant more poplars and willows in the home valleys, I thought to myself.

Back over the boundary fence and onto the better formed track, still remnants of the old bridle path, low banks to our left, hand-hewn, another two kilometres to the ATV and a welcome sit-down. Walking is a highlight of this extensive type of farming we do, but it's always a relief to stop and take a load off, and right now, after hours on my pins, sitting was what I needed. Gammy leg needing a rest and me trying to ignore it. Weak-kneed prick.

Liz saw them first. She was ahead of me, not far, just out to my right and off the walking track. She stopped, stared and so did I. Across the bends of the creek, walking briskly our way, were two people: a woman and her companion, a man carrying a shoulder-slung rifle.

II

Liz growled.

"Settle, Gretel," I told her, being a bit casual with names as I'm wont to be. "It's a free world." We were on a public walking track after all.

The man spotted us at about 200 metres, pretty much at the same time as we saw them, and grabbed the woman's elbow. The pair slowed down and began to talk. I called Liz to get in behind and continued along the track, noticing that I was limping perceptibly now. There were people about to see so I made an effort to walk properly.

Liz wanted to bounce ahead and check them out but I kept her in behind, as her friendly smile was often taken by unsuspecting people as a snarl or grimace. Murray had taught her to do the ugly smile on command for a laugh, and it worked for most people who knew her well.

As we rounded another bend I saw they were youngish, mid-twenties perhaps, clearly not dressed for tramping or hunting. No decent boots. Track shoes, jeans, windbreakers, city-style backpacks. They appeared still hesitant about coming forward, and were talking rapidly between themselves.

They were unknown to me, which meant nothing, as there are always strangers on this track, usually trampers and tourists from all over. During the summer this was regarded as one of the country's most interesting walkways because of its isolation and its history of abandoned settlements — it had been called the Valley of Broken Dreams. A day's walk would bring you to the famous Bridge to Nowhere, a too-late attempt in the 1930s Depression to provide improved access for the settlers. The track was featured in all the guidebooks and was quite popular as a result.

Liz, ignoring me, bounded forward and pranced around the pair as they stopped and waited for me to come to them. When I got there Liz stopped running around their legs and waited, rapt as the woman reached down and patted her sleek sides, talking dog to her. The bloke meanwhile was clearly uncomfortable, meeting my eyes then looking away in every direction including at his feet. Not aggressive, more surprised, confused maybe. His right hand reached up and grasped the rifle barrel behind his shoulder.

"Gidday," I said. "Don't worry about the dog, she'd lick you to death. Get in behind, Liz."

The woman straightened up and moved closer to the man, and they both looked at me. Unsure of what to do next.

"We didn't expect to see anyone here today," the man said.

He unslung the rifle awkwardly, put its butt on the ground. "Anybody else about?" he asked.

"No, you've got the track to yourself this afternoon," I replied, and tried not to look at the rifle, which I knew at a glance was my own. I always carry a small Ruger with me on the ATV, a .22 Magnum to knock off goats and hares which are a nuisance on the farm. When I'd set off to walk this morning I had left the rifle in its carrier and taken only a ski pole with me for walking stability. It was a strongly constructed yet lightweight rifle, ideal to carry outside in the rough. It never rusted or rotted.

"Where are you heading?" I asked, just for something to say, because it was bloody obvious. At the next junction along the track, four hours away, they could only turn left to the nearest small town, Raetihi, or right towards the Mangapurua

Valley and the Bridge to Nowhere, and they were hardly equipped or likely to be going in that direction.

"Raetihi," the man replied.

The woman stared hard at him and spoke as if I wasn't there.

"We'll have to shoot him," she said.

Bugger this, I thought, and looked at the bank beside me, then sat down on it, bringing my pole between my boots to lean forward on. I'm no brave bastard, that's for sure, and normally this approach or attitude would have scared me witless. I had a little edge, though, on this occasion. The Magnum used a nine-shot revolving magazine — and it was safely in my pocket. Leaving a rifle in plain sight is one thing. Leaving a rifle in plain sight, loaded, was quite another.

With the sharp point of my ski pole I was as well armed as they were, especially as Liz would probably bite someone quite savagely if they got aggressive towards me.

"Shoot me! What the hell's this? This is my land here, a public track, a decent sort of day. Shoot me! That would really piss me off."

"I'm sorry," said the bloke, having the decency to look it. "We're in deep shit, and meeting you wasn't part of our plan. In fact, meeting you here has stuffed us up, good and proper."

These people were confused. It dawned on me why I wasn't scared. This couple, despite their words and their obvious nerves, didn't look threatening. Like most people, I have in my time come across the odd lowlife, and in my younger days I've been in situations I had wished I wasn't. This somehow wasn't like that. These people, rifle and all, were more scared of me than I was of them.

"Look," I replied, adopting as friendly but firm a tone as I thought I could get away with, "you'd better tell me what the heck you're up to. In fact tell me what you're up to and I'll level with you. A blind man could see you don't know what you are doing." This area of remote rugged National Park is popular amongst hunters and some of our neighbours as a crafty place away from it all to grow certain illegal crops, but these two didn't look the types for that either.

Growing dak has been, to my observation, the preserve of the sort of drongos my long-departed mother would have kindly called 'ne'er-do-wells'.

They looked at each other in confusion. Wanting to talk about me and not wanting to. Wanting to talk to me and not being able to. Shit, I'm getting soft, I'll have to help them along, I thought.

"I'll tell you what," I started. "If it makes it any easier for you, Liz here's actually a man-eater. She only looks placid." The woman giggled and looked grateful for a second for lightening their load. Really though. "I live here, my name's Tony Price, the rifle you are holding is actually mine and before you find out by accident, it's not loaded." The man's mouth gaped as open as the breech on the rifle and his eyes widened then looked down; he clearly knew nothing of firearms.

"We know who you are." He was still staring down at the rifle, wondering why he had bothered to take it at all, I suppose.

"Sit down, take a break," I said. "You guys owe me an explanation here. You've threatened to knock me off out in the middle of nowhere, you've pinched my rifle, and you look to be ever so slightly out of your depth in some mess or another. No matter what you've heard, I'm not a total ratbag. Tell me what's going on and let's see what's best to do."

III

The woman now looked close to tears. Sat down on the bank ten feet away and looked back along where they had come from. The man shifted from foot to foot, then moved forward and leant against the bank halfway between me and the woman. Shoved his hands deep in his pockets, as if to brace himself.

Slight but wiry of build, it was easy to see he was close to losing the plot. His eyes moved from staring down to looking at me fleetingly, then his woman, then me, then down again. Times like this, the thought flashed through my mind, I wished I still smoked. Rolling gives your hands and eyes something to do in awkward pauses. Kills you in the long run, but saves the moment.

"I'm … I'm one of the Applebys," the young man said. Shit, one of that sad tribe. A whole heap of negative thought raced through my mind. I sighed and looked up at him.

"Yeah, I know you've no time for us," he muttered.

"That may be true," I replied, "but I've never seen you before in my life."

Old man Appleby was a clever bastard. He and his brood, a daughter, two sons, and a wife of sorts had moved in up the road eight years before. The community, such as remains here, made them welcome, hands-off with rural reserve, but genuinely welcome. Their farm was a block of reverted scrub, old collapsed totara fences, and rumours. Rumours because they always lived beyond their evident means, their visible means of support, and appeared to do nothing, nothing physical that is. Appleby was one of those people who, if he put his brains to work constructively, could have been a wealthy man. Everything that went wrong in his life he predictably maintained was the fault of someone else. He spent his life in a battle against everybody in authority and, in fact, everybody he came in contact with.

After a year or two in the district his kids had left home — driven out, was the local version. Harassed sexually was an easy rumour, as he had always talked smut. Not to the men, of course. I made the mistake early in the piece of seeing him standing alone at a local do and approaching him to make conversation. I quickly realised why he was usually alone in public. He never had anything positive to say for himself. Invective. Everyone was behind a plot to bring him to his knees. From where, I was never sure. He never gave up angling to get the female members of any group into private conversation, but was avoided as all the women, and even school-age girls, soon found his mind had a single track which led only to remarks about their physical attributes.

People, bless them, are usually optimists so they would swing in support of his wife. We soon realised, however, that having spent most of her life with him she had ended up as bent as he was.

So here I was faced with a son I hardly knew existed, who was obviously in something up to his eyes and didn't know what to do about it.

When he finally started speaking to me the words came in a torrent. "I'm Brent Appleby, this is Jan, my wife. We haven't been home since I left when I was fifteen. The old lady wrote and asked me to come back and make up with them. I was reluctant, didn't ever want to see the old bastard again. I'd even changed my name by deed poll to Appleton to break the family connection.

"Jan, though, had never met my parents and couldn't see the harm in a weekend visit. Not her fault. I'd been away fourteen years and thought the old man might have changed. No chance. Randy old rooster. We'd only been here a couple of hours and he was hitting on Jan.

"How do you explain to someone that your own flesh and blood are such skungy people? I mean, I'd told her about them, why I'd left home, why I wouldn't invite them to our wedding, why I wouldn't bring the kids to meet them. But the reality of her actually meeting them was too tough."

"His reputation locally isn't that flash," I reflected.

"Not flash!" Brent Appleby/Appleton snarled. "I left home because he was a boy botherer and general sex fiend. I've been home hardly more than a day and he was after my wife. Un-bloody-believable. The old bastard is seventy and he's still as horny as a cane toad. He was disgusting."

"You've been living in Aussie," I said, realising from his choice of metaphor and slight accent.

"Brisbane." Jan spoke for the first time in a while.

"Just go back, forget them, go back to your own life and forget they ever existed," I said.

"That was the plan," Brent replied. "We just didn't count on meeting you."

"So what's the harm?" I couldn't see how meeting me was so bad.

"I killed them," he said.

"*We* killed them," Jan said quickly, wanting immediately to share the blame.

"Fuck a duck, you're serious?"

IV

Brent Appleby sat down with a thump between me and his wife, beside the rifle but not touching it. Jan sat there hugging her knees and he leaned forward, looking at her. She stretched up, leant back a little and looked directly at me for the first time.

"We flew over from home the day before yesterday," she explained. "Brent's parents met us at Taupo airport and drove us to the farm. Brent didn't want to come back; now I know why. We'd only been there since Friday, catching up, having cups of tea and so on. He really is … was … a horny little prick. The second Brent was out of the room this morning he came in leering and groping at me, asking 'Was I getting enough?' Christ, what did I do to deserve that?"

"Brent came back in, saw the expression on my face and knew straight away. He grabbed me, grabbed our backpacks and stormed out. The sleazy shit charged after us, calling us names I'd never heard. Ranting and bloody raving. Totally off his trolley."

"He's always had the reputation of being a few sheep short in his top paddock," I offered lamely, then hooked right in. "So what happened then? You were leaving …"

Brent took up the story, his voice a monotone. "He stormed after us, right down the drive, and followed us onto the bridge. Halfway over he lunged at Jan, grabbed her shoulder and pulled her towards him. I lost it. As he turned Jan around I broke him away and flung him around and he went over the side. The old lady came up screaming abuse, hysterically flailing at me, so I didn't have time to think, I tried to deflect her and in pushing her off me, she went over too. It all happened in a flash."

Christ on a crutch! I knew the Applebys' bridge. It stood, or rather leaned, thirty metres above a deep pool in an otherwise shallow river.

"They just lay still and lifeless, and slowly floated away. We stood there, gasping. There wasn't a flicker of life in their bodies. They just drifted away." His face was white as he told the story, reliving each moment.

We all sat quietly for what seemed like ages, just looking at each other. No wonder these poor critters didn't know what to do. Who would? They would be feeling every rotten emotion known to humanity, but my first reaction was that they had done us all a service. Everyone had thought for years the Applebys were a waste of skin, but rather than shatter the peace they had stayed out of their lives. Small rural communities have to do that. You either confront issues head-on and risk becoming unpopular, or become apathetic. The latter's easier.

We looked at each other. I grinned. Just a little grin. There had to be a way out of this. Now, I'm not a great judge of character, but I've met people who are. Old Tom Ngatai who used to drive my bulldozer could sum a person up accurately after a few minutes, but not me. Neither could Georgina. We always like to give a person the benefit of charity. And we're often wrong. And we hadn't learnt not to in thirty years.

This pair clearly weren't evil, though. Confused, shocked, bewildered, murderers even, but not that bad. This event was much more like manslaughter. Their first misfortune was Brent coming from trash parents. They had got away; their second misfortune was coming back.

"You actually just flicked them over the bridge rails?" My

voice wavered between amusement and incredulity. "Was there anybody about?"

Brent looked at me again. "You know, I'd never completely written off the old lady since I cleared out. But it came to me in a flash that she was just as bad as the old man. Her turning a blind eye to his evil ways for all those years. She was just as bad. No, no one saw. She said we were their first visitors for weeks. She said no one around here talks to them any more. No one knew we were staying there. They hadn't told neighbours we were coming home because no one talked to them. We were just going to walk away. Hitch south from Raetihi and pretend we hadn't been there. Then you came along …

"Yeah, I was fuming. I just grabbed the old bastard and swung him round. He hit the rail, flipped forward and kept turning over and over until he struck the water. With old lady, she went berserk. I was just trying to fend her off."

Time for a decision or two. Someone was likely to be looking for me, and more Prices here right now would only make matters more complicated.

"Okay," I said, talking quickly. "Here's a plan. I can't imagine what crap you young Applebys have put up with from childhood. You just keep on walking. I won't say anything. Give me a contact number, no, ring me, ring me and say you can't reach your folks. So you can keep in touch. I hope you're right and no one saw you; I've no reason to suspect you're not right. Just walk away. Who's to say it wasn't suicide?" I said, thinking ahead as I talked. "Let's just wait and see what happens."

They sat there, the expression on their faces relaxing, but still unsure what to do. Unsure that they could really trust me.

Reading their thoughts, I said, "I won't report you or say anything. Letting you go means I've probably compromised myself, for one thing.

"You won't realise this now but you've done the world a favour. You've suffered from your parents, so have your brother and sister, so has everyone that's come into contact with them. So have my family. There'll be no shortage of people with a motive. Also, they won't be missed for a while. Go, clear off out of here, ring me in a couple of weeks.

"I'll go home and wait. No sense me doing anything until there's something to react to."

They stood up. I pushed myself to my feet as well. The distrust between us had eased. We turned to go our own ways.

Jan first. "Are you sure this is a good idea?"

"No," I replied, "but we've gotta pull finger, and it looks okay from where I'm standing."

Brent too looked undecided, but was keener to skedaddle. "Sorry about the gun," he said. "Thanks, I think you're right, we'll get out of here."

He turned to his wife, took her elbow and looked straight at her. "It'll all work out okay. Mr Price is right, they won't be missed. They said it themselves. The old lady said on the way home, they only stay in one place until they've fallen out with everybody, but they stayed on here after that."

He turned, thanked me again, and they walked off. Slowly at first, then faster as they realised they could be free.

Their path, even in the twilight, would be clearly defined and they would be unnoticed as they made their way south.

"Come on, Lizard," I said, and set off the other way. "Let's go home and have a cup of tea."

V

Walking's a bloody marvellous tonic. I'm no health fanatic, I just enjoy it. And it gives a man time to think.

With our place consisting of four full-time family members working we have an 'open idea' policy. In other words, if your idea's got merit, let's do it that way for a change. Never mind the way I've done it for thirty years. Equally, and to that end, we have regular family meetings where we discuss everything to do with running the farm, and our lives together, successfully. Sort of getting on but not being in each other's pockets. Quite a fine line between getting along swimmingly and driving each other nuts. As I walked, I thought of the approach I should take when I got home.

First up, I'd have to change the habit of a lifetime, and say nothing to the family. Compromising myself was one thing, I thought, compromising the others wouldn't be bright. I would say nothing and wait and see what developed.

Sometimes I even discussed my ideas with Liz, but not this one. In any case she was sauntering along beside me as though nothing out of the ordinary had just happened.

I reached my mud-caked ATV at last, re-secured the rifle on the rack behind the bench seat, hopped in and turned homeward. I'd only gone half a kilometre when Jack arrived on his bike to see where I was.

Brief greeting. "Everything sweet?"

"Yep, walked right around that block," I waved with a wide scoop of my arm to where I'd been earlier, "and along the

Kaiwhakauku track for a while. Found another four cows." I told him where. "Let's go home, I'm as dry as a witch's tit."

Jack turned and raced off as I bounced along at my usual, more sedate pace. Liz stood on the deck behind me, peering around my back to look ahead.

I still felt uneasy as I drove into the yard. Something momentous had happened to me, yet I'd just committed myself to going home and carrying on as though nothing out of the ordinary had gone on. Unnatural. When really I was bursting to share my experiences and new-found knowledge.

I mucked around in the shed for a few minutes before going into the house, even though I was starting to get hungry. Fuelled the bike for the next day, strolled to the house, kicked off my boots, stepped inside to put the billy on.

"How did you get on?" Georgina called out from the sewing room.

"Not too bad. Found another four cows and the rest won't be far away. Cup of tea?"

I made two cups and wandered in to see what she was up to. Watched for a while as she laid out colourful pieces of patterned fabric on the floor like a jigsaw. Quilting, more of a passion than a hobby.

Then I strolled out the back door and around the deck. I never tired of the familiar view of our garden oaks and copper beeches giving way to mahoe and kowhai above the broad, slow-moving expanse of water down the Whanganui. I could see for a kilometre until the river passed round the bend by Wade's Landing, where the riverboats used to call. Stood there on the verandah, wondering if the bodies had floated past this very point.

*

The next day, Monday, we all had breakfast together at seven, our regular meeting to discuss the week ahead.

This week we had TB testing. Mustering all our cattle three months old and over for their annual test. New Zealand has had a bovine tuberculosis problem for years. Mainly spread by possums, feral deer and farmers moving livestock around the country before the days of movement control restrictions.

The testing is an unproductive task — three days working for no income. It's just a job that has to be done. To make it more worthwhile we try to do something else with the cattle while they are in the yards, like giving them a drench, copper injection or sometimes pregnancy testing if the TB test coincides with the correct time of the year. Pregnancy testing, or its more modern replacement, ultrasonic scanning, has to happen at around two months after the bulls have been with the cows.

So Monday this week was all-day mustering for TB testing on Tuesday. Then the cattle would wait around in holding paddocks near the yards until the test was read on Friday, before being taken back to paddocks further out in the hills.

We had a satisfactory muster with all the cows rounded up, including the extras I'd seen on my Sunday walk. All the yearling bulls, heifers and steers came in as well, along with a mob of fattening heifers.

Tuesday started bright and early for the boys to have all the cattle in the two sets of yards, ready to go through once the AgriQuality livestock inspector arrived.

I was to wait around home until he turned up, to take him out to the yards and help push the cattle through.

"You're early, Bruce." I greeted our regular inspector when he drove up at 8.30 rather than the appointed 9 a.m.

"Your neighbours up the valley didn't have their cattle in," replied Bruce, sounding peeved. "Second time this year I've arranged to be there. Even rang to remind them a few days ago, bloody typical.

"They only have fifty-odd head of cattle, I don't know why they can't be bothered. It just costs them more for me to make a special trip back."

I offered him a cup of tea, but he bustled around organising his gear. He wanted to get going so that his entire morning wouldn't be wasted. We tied his bag of tricks — vials of tuberculin, injecting gun, gloves and ear-tags and other tools — on the ATV's deck and trundled off to our main cattle yards.

Bruce is normally a cheerful bloke, happy in his work. Having the Applebys not bother to muster their cattle to test he took as a personal insult, so I was glad of the bike noise making conversation more difficult. I couldn't understand his mutterings. And driving the vehicle gave me something to be busy doing, to avoid saying more than I had to.

By the time all our cattle had been put through the race and Bruce and the boys had a cuppa together at the yards, he had resumed his more usual affable manner and didn't mention the Applebys again. None of us did, so to my relief everything continued as though nothing untoward had happened.

VI

Wednesday and Thursday's challenges were moving mobs of ewes about their winter rotations, fence maintenance (which was this winter's priority 'in-between' job), and not thinking about anything that was happening outside our front gate.

Friday, Bruce was back to read the test of our cattle. At the first run-through on the Tuesday he had injected a minute amount of tuberculin, a sterile solution derived from the TB bacterium, into the rump of each beast. Four days later, if there was any swelling where he made the injection, the animal was deemed to be a reactor, to have bovine TB. It was immediately identified as such with a special tag and removed from the mob to be slaughtered. At the freezing works there would be a further post-mortem inspection for visible lesions.

Not once had we ever had a reactor, not since testing began in 1967. But it was always a little tense as the last cattle were pushed through the race and their tails felt at the fold where the tail joins the body. Clear once more — our clean status confirmed. It only remained to put the cattle out of the holding paddocks.

I drove Bruce back to the house to have lunch and complete the paperwork. It's a bugger, but it has to be done.

"Still no one home at Applebys," said Bruce. "I dropped off a re-test notice in their mailbox and it's full of mail and milk. Hasn't been cleared for days." He scrubbed his boots, as always, and came over to the house. "Must have cleared off for a few days," he suggested, and didn't mention them again.

Another week over, another weekend passed uneventfully. Campbell and Murray took the jetboat out for a while on Saturday to go pig hunting down river, to give their dogs a run. I wondered privately how they would react to finding the odd floating body, but dismissed the thought after imagining that the bodies were already out to sea and probably disposed of by sharks or sea lice. I estimated that, given a clear run, it could take as little as two or three days for a body to float all the way down to the Tasman.

Sure, they could have been spotted by a passing boatie or canoeist, but there was every possibility that they could float unnoticed all the way.

Monday brought a discussion with the boys about sheep. Ewes, actually. Every year we set out a precise number of ewes in each paddock at least two weeks before they are due to start lambing. This gives them time to settle in, to find their way around, to realise they aren't going to be moved every three days. We separate those having twins from those having single lambs, which we know from scanning back in June. Then we give them a vaccination for five serious lurgies that affect them or their lambs. The numbers per paddock I've worked out simply through experience. Trial and error. The twinning ewes need more grass and more gently contoured paddocks.

We were going well. We'd built a double drenching race system and were pumping quite a few sheep through when two policemen turned up. Hardly a common occurrence in these parts. We all downed tools as they walked through the gates from the ute they had parked on the driveway.

"How's it going? You look a tad busy," said the older of the two. Both constables, as I couldn't see any stripes, and they were in uniform. In their shiny shoes they stepped gingerly across the yard to where we were hanging up our gear.

"Yeah, gidday," said Campbell, ever sociable and ready to give a bit of cheek. "You guys want a job?"

"You'd be happy as, drenching these sheep, if you had to do some of the jobs we have to," said the older cop.

"What's up, men?" I asked. Then said to the boys, "Let's go and have a cup of tea, seeing it looks like we've stopped."

Letting Brent and Jan Appleby walk away and keeping quiet about what they had done had seemed a good idea at the time, but now that the police were here I wasn't sure which way to look. Trying to appear nonchalant, to avoid looking nervous.

We all moved through the waiting ewes to the back of the yards, out onto the grass, to head towards the house.

"Have you seen anything of Mr and Mrs Appleby lately?" the first policeman asked as we walked past the shed.

The boys didn't respond immediately and nor did I. Then Jack volunteered, "We don't see them much in the normal run of things; they keep fairly much to themselves."

"Yes, we've gathered in the past that they wouldn't win any popularity contests down here," said the older officer.

We arrived at the porch and stooped to undo our boots. Kicked them off and washed our hands and arms in the sink outside the laundry. Then walked into the kitchen and greeted Georgina, "Tea for ten, sweet thing."

Not one to be unaware of what was happening on the farm, Georgina already had the jug on and was fishing around in the pantry for anything that our gannet-gutted sons had left untouched this morning.

She came out grinning with a large tin and greeted the policemen. "Hello, come in and sit down. Tea or coffee?"

The older policeman had been taken along with the flow of things and decided it was time to get a bit more serious.

"Coffee for us please, Mrs Price. I'm Joe Webb and this is Peter Cochrane. We're from Taumarunui. We've been asked to see the Applebys in connection with an enquiry, couldn't get them on the phone this morning, so we rang the Durhams across from them. Charlie Durham went over and couldn't see a soul around the house, so he rang back and said the place looks abandoned. The boss sent us down to look around."

Jack, Campbell and Murray settled down behind the long rimu kitchen table, I sat on the other side and the two policemen sat down either side of me. Then Murray got up and busied himself getting mugs together while Georgina put sugar and milk on the table.

Campbell reached across for the tin, but without turning around Georgina anticipated him. "Put them on a plate, please Campbell," which he did, with a grin.

"They could be anywhere on their place," Campbell offered. "I mean, it's quite big." He meant big and scrub-covered and was too polite to say so.

"Yes, they could," said Joe Webb, "and we haven't been on the property at all yet. But around the house it does look deserted, and there's a week's mail in their box."

Murray reached for a biscuit. "Last year when I was over there to drop off a couple of their double-deckers ..." — he was referring to sheep with two years' wool on them that had strayed onto our place — "... there was a dog or two in kennels behind the woolshed. Are they still there, and have they been fed?"

"Didn't look," said Joe. He leant back and looked at his mate. "It would only take you ten minutes to get back and have a look."

Joe must be a senior constable. The younger man pushed his chair back, quickly put his shoes on, jogged over to their ute and was off up the road.

While we waited we didn't talk of the Applebys but of

the usual rural things like the weather, the All Blacks, the condition of the road. And of the work ahead.

I wasn't used to keeping things from my wife for so long. Wasn't used to not looking directly at people. Let alone Georgina. We had always known instinctively that talking everything over made our lives easier. To have not done so was to change a habit of thirty years.

Fortunately we didn't have long to sit around.

VII

The police ute came back at a rate faster than most of us drive around here. Pulled up again by the woolshed, and Peter policeman was back to the house before his coffee had gone cold.

"There's one dog there," he said, not even short of breath. "It looks as though it's been given a full carcass of something, a few days ago. There's a full backbone by his kennel and bits of skin everywhere. He's not happy though, and I couldn't see any water."

"Poor mutt," said Campbell, who loves his dogs. "What about the other kennels?" He offered to bring the dog home for a while so it could be fed and watered regularly.

"It doesn't look as though either of the other kennels have been used for ages," Peter answered. "Unless there's another place where the Applebys tie dogs up, there's only one dog."

"Is their car in the shed?" Georgina asked.

"What about bikes?" Jack chipped in. "I'm sure they have had a four-wheeler."

"Yes, their car's there. Or at least there's a white car there," said Joe. "The garage door's closed and will take some opening. The door's off its hinges and the whole shed's quite rickety."

It dawned on me that these were not rural coppers, and not from a rural background. "Look," I said, "go back over, check their animals, dogs or dog, give him some water. Check for cats, chooks, pets, have a look around. We'll get our job under way again and one or two of us can come over with the bikes if you come back and tell us what's going on."

"Fair enough," Joe said. "Can you make any suggestion as to where we should look?"

"None of us go over there much," Georgina offered diplomatically. "We did for a while, but weren't exactly made welcome."

"Queer bastards, I reckon," Campbell didn't often hold back his opinions. I frowned at him and he grinned back. "Well, they are, aren't they?"

The policemen thanked Georgina for the refreshments and put their not-so-shiny shoes back on. We pulled on our boots and walked back to their ute with them.

"They'll be there somewhere," Campbell said. "They've often had bailiffs after them, so they're masters of the disappearing act." We had all heard stories of Applebys being pursued for debt on a regular basis.

"Come back if you need a hand," I said again as I watched them leave. "We'll be right here most of today."

We carried on vaccinating our ewes. After another few races full Murray and Jack took the first fifteen hundred away to their lambing paddocks. Campbell and I carried on, concentrating on our job. It's precise work, putting a needle in a sheep's neck in the correct place every time. We worked for a while quietly, each of us no doubt having distinctly different thoughts about what would happen next. Relaxing and going with the flow still seemed the best option for me.

"What's going on with them, do you reckon?" Campbell asked as we started on two more full races.

"Hard to know." I leaned back and stretched my aching muscles to gain a moment to think. "I've never known what they get up to over there."

The place had been a dump as long as I could remember. Most farmers, most landowners and householders, knew that keeping their assets looking sharp gave as satisfying a return on investment as we would ever achieve. The Applebys were the exception. Their house, their farm and their stock reflected the way they really were. They had delusions that they were competent farmers but did nothing to maintain standards, let alone improve them.

Soon the police ute came back again and Joe stopped long enough to call out that they wanted to use our phone. We waved them on and continued our work.

After another quarter of an hour they were back and stopped to tell us what they had discovered.

"There doesn't look to have been anyone there for days," Joe began. "It looks like they just walked out and didn't come back. The car's there, there's an old but serviceable ATV in a lean-to, it looks like the only one. I just rang the boss in town to explain it as I see it. He's suggested getting a couple of your guys to ride around the farm tracks with us to see what we can see. How are you placed?"

"Good as wood," I said. "As soon as Murray and Jack come back, any minute now, we can come over on the bikes and drive you over the place."

"Great," said Joe. "The alternatives are either getting stuck in this ute or getting a helicopter. The boss thinks the helicopter's a bit premature. Mostly in cases like this people just wander back home. Don't know though, the place certainly looks abandoned."

We stopped work as we finished the races we were working on so we could give the police our full attention.

"Campbell, you go and check the fuel in our bikes, grab some coats so these guys don't freeze to death and as soon as the others get back, shoot through." Though the worst of winter was probably over, you needed to be prepared for any sort of weather in country like this.

Jack and Campbell took off with a policeman each, and

Murray and I vaccinated the remaining ewes and sent them away.

We returned home on dark and dealt with the dogs. Letting the pups out of their run, cutting up goat meat and feeding chunks of it to all the dogs, around twenty at the moment, then locking them up again took a good half hour each evening.

We were still unlacing our boots on the porch when the searchers returned. The boys had taken a comprehensive look-see around the buildings and surroundings for a while with the police, then been for a long ride around all the navigable tracks they could find. None of them had seen a thing of interest.

The boys, always on the lookout for the tracks of feral deer and pigs, weren't trackers in the Aboriginal sense of the word, but they were observant as rural dwellers tend to be. Neither son had seen any fresh or even recent tyre marks or footprints where they had ridden. The few stock the Applebys owned used the same tracks to go from each open patch of grass to the next and would wipe out anything not newish.

We settled around the kitchen table again to discuss what to do next. The three young farmers made straight for the beer fridge as young men are liable to do, while the policemen opted for another coffee. I decided though that the occasion called for a decent slug of whisky to contemplate the situation with. The night before I'd needed several to put myself to sleep. The boys were all snoring off comfortably in their houses and Georgina had worn herself out with her busy day in the house and around the farm, but at 11.30 I had found myself staring at the dying embers in the fireplace, wide awake with worry. The whisky didn't give me any answers but it helped me forget the questions.

Joe and Peter had obviously enjoyed their afternoon ride and were amazed where the 4 x 4 ATVs would go. Which made me even more pleased I'd stayed home. They summed the situation as they saw it.

"It looks as though no one has seen either Mr or Mrs Appleby for six or seven days," Joe started. "Could even be ten. There are certainly five daily papers in their mailbox. There's no one anywhere around the house or sheds, and there hasn't been for a while. There's no one anywhere obvious around the farm."

Campbell had other ideas. "We only saw a quarter of it. There are huge areas not covered by the tracks." He looked across at me. "Have you still got that aerial photo?"

"Sure, I think so," I said, and got up to have a look. I had an old Regional Council photo of most of our valley, showing five or six farms in black and white. I dug it out of a tube in the office and unrolled it on the table, holding the corners down with the boys' beer bottles.

Campbell pointed out to the policemen where they had just come back from searching. The photo was quite old but on a small scale it showed up clearly the vast areas of the Appleby property not tracked or developed. Their farm had had about five owners since around 1910 when it was first broken in. In earlier years it had been well developed to pasture land, as the photo showed. Large areas of regrowth scrub showed up quite differently from standing bush.

The police were obviously surprised at how little they had seen from their long ride, and how much more there was to cover by foot or air if any thorough search were to be made.

Joe asked to use the phone again. Their mobiles or ute radio wouldn't get a signal in our valley. It was either landline or carrier pigeon.

We sipped our drinks as we listened to Joe describing to someone senior in town what they had discovered, or hadn't. He spoke highly of the boys' co-operation in showing them around, and went on to describe all the land they had yet to see. He detailed exactly what they had observed around the homestead and suggested options: ground search, heli-search or both. He hung up the phone after a while and turned to us.

"How many people could we get to help with a ground search?"

Between us we replied by counting available bodies from here back to the main highway, 18 kilometres away. Depends who's doing what, we agreed.

"Around ten men, that's leaving two of us here to carry on with the farm work, and two of us to help," I summed up. "We can all go, if you think it's warranted."

"Don't think so," Joe replied. "Ten of you, four of us. If we could find a decent map or photo, would that be enough?"

Back to the photo we went to divide what we could see of the place into blocks. Not really enough men, was the consensus.

"But in a whole day we could cover a hell of a lot."

Second question from Joe. "Where would we find an up-to-date map or photo?" We all agreed on the Council, which we always suspected of photographing the whole region regularly to keep a check on what we were up to.

"Okay," said Joe. "The boss thinks a ground search first. We'll ring around for local volunteers who have a fair chance of knowing the place at least a little. I'll try Rodney Buckland at the Council tonight for a photo. If we could meet at Applebys' tomorrow at, say, nine in the morning, send out some people to specific areas and see what we can come up with. If that fails we'll call in a helicopter for any bits we may have missed.

"So, can you commit to two men from 9 a.m. till about 4 p.m.? We want everyone out long before dark." Joe was thinking on his feet.

Georgina, who had been working in the kitchen, came over with a pad and pen. She and the boys quickly drew up a list of potential volunteers for the police to call. Joe watched as Georgina and the boys coupled people with bikes.

"Can I ring them now? We're an hour from town. If I can do it from here we'll all know where we stand."

He took the list, the local directory and the portable phone and sat down a little away from us. While he rang around, the boys replaced their beers and Jack refreshed my whisky. Talking quietly amongst ourselves, it was soon obvious from our crew that volunteers to go weren't a problem. Who would stay home would be, until Georgina said bluntly, "All of you go. This could be nothing, or it could be serious." She looked at me. "You stick to the open country, you boys do the rough stuff and if they are there you'll soon find them." And thus it was decided.

Joe soon finished his phoning and came over to us, pleasantly surprised. "What's up here? Everyone's keen as hell to help."

"Curiosity," I told him. "The Apples have been a bloody mystery for years. No one's ever got familiar with them after the first setback, but everyone's wondered how they keep going. There's been lots of talk. How many have you ended up with?"

Joe looked up from the list he was showing Peter. "Twelve men and ten ATVs."

Small communities usually rally together when they are needed. Partly from a sense of civic responsibility, but also because it's an interesting break from day-to-day life. One example I'd noted before was that we often consider ourselves too busy to use the jetboat as much as we would like, but if someone comes in or rings up wanting rescuing, we're all off like a shot. Spontaneous boating trips, like spontaneous parties, are often the best.

We changed our week's plans, leaving them flexible, and the boys went to their respective houses to eat and sleep. Tomorrow could be a big day.

VIII

Next morning we started at daylight to knock off a couple of little jobs that couldn't wait — closing a few gates behind the sheep we'd let out the day before and shifting some cows to a fresh paddock. We fuelled our bikes, tied on wet-weather gear and lunch boxes and set off at about quarter to nine. While the days were drawing out a bit, this was the King Country in the late winter — another overcast sky, with fog that would lie in the valleys for hours after sunrise. Still cool enough to wrap up with warm windproof clothing before setting out on a long bike ride. I know they're ATVs and we often call them that or by their brand names — mine's a Polaris — but we also still call them bikes because they're not much more than a four-wheel bike with a cab on, open on both sides. They can shiver your goolies off on a cold day.

The scene that greeted us on the road outside the Applebys' front gate was a surprise. The dozen locals who had volunteered the previous evening were all there. Those who were neighbours we knew well, but in addition there were another ten of the alternative lifestyle brigade who live between here and the main road.

The rural population has shrunk worldwide in developed countries for 100 years, so it's no new phenomenon. The reasons are many and varied. I suppose technology is responsible. Replacing teams of men with scythes, using instead one man with a tractor and mower; mechanising shearing and other labour-intensive jobs, the list goes on. When you combine the mechanical revolution with successive governments' inability to control inflation, the economies of scale affecting farms have changed over recent decades. The 1000-ewe farm of the 1940s needed to be a 3000 stock unit farm in the 1980s, and probably a 5000 stock unit farm by year 2000. Larger farms have been created by buying out neighbours, with one of the results being a surplus of rural housing. There has been a drift of rural people to the towns and cities, but also a small reverse drift back to the valleys, with quite a few looking for a cheap house to rent where they can have an alternative lifestyle.

By and large, these people have been an asset to the communities in that their children have boosted school rolls, resisting the closure of many marginally viable schools. Their casual labour has also been keenly sought in busy seasons and their tenancies have stopped many houses falling into disrepair. A few locals, not so charitably, thought they were purely here to grow dope in the remote valleys, and maybe a few of them were. On our place our minds were open. As long as they didn't grow dope on our land or try to sell it to our kids, we couldn't care less.

Ten people had turned up without being asked, and by the grins on greetings between friends and neighbours they were relishing the thought of a legitimate nosy around a farm the community were curious about.

Joe and Peter were there talking casually and soon, as we milled about, another police Land Cruiser drew up. A middle-aged sergeant hopped out, dressed in practical police-issue clothes more like search and rescue gear than formal uniform, including long boots. He pulled on a heavy fleece-lined coat, slammed his door and, with a younger policewoman, came to join us. He spent a few minutes with Joe and Peter, then came over to me.

"Thanks for your help yesterday," he said, introducing

himself as Malcolm Bryant and his offsider, whose name I didn't catch.

"No worries," said Jack, to whom nothing much was a worry.

With a friendly grin he turned to the farmers and others and welcomed us there. "Thanks very much for coming," he said. "To save wasting time I'll draw up a grid to allocate people to set areas. That way we will get the property covered as quickly and efficiently as possible. Now, to help with that, who knows the place best?"

Years before we came here, others owned or grazed the Appleby property, so without any fuss we nominated another neighbour, Fred Clarke. He and his wife had tried harder than most to be good neighbours to the Apples and before his time, his father Bert had grazed the place between owners.

Fred came forward and we gathered around the bonnet of the police ute as Joe rolled out a large colour photo of the Appleby farm. Malcolm Bryant took charge again, found a pen to use as a pointer and asked Fred to explain where we were standing. Fred leaned closer and gave up immediately. "I can't bloody see that," he said, patting his pockets. "Didn't think I'd need my glasses."

Joe immediately suggested Jack, who'd been around the farm with him the previous evening. Jack came forward reluctantly and pointed out where we were standing, the boundaries, and tracks they had gone over yesterday. Between his contribution and Malcolm's, lines were soon drawn down ridges dissecting the place, and ten roughly equal areas drawn up.

He then did a quick head count and began to sort out the ATVs.

"Look, this may not agree with you all, but here's my suggestion. Each ATV should only take two people max; they were really only made to carry one. So I'll give each ATV driver an area to search; each of us from the police will go on a bike, so the other drivers can choose six companions. The rest of you are really surplus to requirements at the moment, I'm afraid. But thanks for coming — Constable Lysaght here will take your names and numbers in case we need to call on you later." He gestured in the direction of the policewoman who had come with him, who was reaching into her pocket for a pad and pen.

There were a few murmurs of disappointment and a little friendly dissent. The people who had come were keyed up for that search and I was on edge myself, half afraid the bodies would be found snagged in fallen branches in the river, half excited that other evidence of Appleby misdemeanors would be uncovered. The extras were in no hurry to go home, so it ended up that a few keen walkers were directed to explore riverbanks and the patches of scrub that were in sight from the buildings. Those on the vehicles would just bypass such places. As an afterthought we had brought our three hand-held mustering radios. The police had four, so seven of us could stay in touch.

"Okay. This sounds like a good plan," Malcolm addressed us all again. "While we're sincerely grateful for you turning up to help, there are a few issues we need to discuss. Firstly and obviously, if you find anything suspicious, please don't touch. I'm not sure what we are looking for. Live people, hopefully. But anything and I mean anything else, please don't touch or even go too close.

"I'd like to think we could all be back here, right on this spot by 3 p.m. If any of you find anything, come out here until you find someone with a radio and we'll take it from there. Be careful, don't get lost yourselves and we will see you all at 3 o'clock."

An air of quiet determination was discernible. Though the searchers were wrapped in beanies, coats and leggings, their eyes were bright and they had the sense of purpose of a bunch of athletes about to start a long race. We sorted ourselves into two men per vehicle, after checking with Malcolm which block each group would be responsible for. The property was around 1200 acres in the old measurement of a flat survey. This meant each of us would be looking closely at less than 100 acres, minus all the open areas you could see over easily. An acre of this sort of rough hill country is much harder to traverse than a similar area of flat land and its broken nature and scattered scrub and bush cover created innumerable potential places of concealment.

The transport started up, set off over the bridge and spread out to go to their designated areas. I'd chosen an easy, rolling area near the centre of the property. The sergeant and I ended up going together, possibly because of our ages. Knowing what I knew, I obviously had a few qualms about being so close to the police while I was probably wasting their time and resources, but at the moment I had little choice but to go with the flow. All things considered, it was possibly the safest place for me to be.

IX

Geologically speaking, this is young country. The base rock, papa, or blue-grey mudstone, is relatively soft and over millions of years water has gouged deep creek and river beds through the valleys. The farms tend to follow the valleys and you can't cross them easily without bridges.

Sergeant Malcolm and I followed along behind the rest until they dispersed and we soon came to the centre of the area we had elected to search. We had chosen well. Within an hour we had walked or ridden over it all and looked fairly closely into the areas that adjoined ours.

Feeling confident we had done our bit, we, like the middle-aged persons we were, rode to higher ground and I dug out my thermos of tea. We could see four of the others and could hear a couple more calling back and forth as they made a thorough investigation of their particular patch of scrub. Malcolm suggested the search wasn't going to take until lunchtime, let alone 3 p.m., but I wasn't so sure. Most of us would finish early but two or three of the more 'upindicular' blocks would take longer. Sure enough, we were joined by two others and then two more who had found nothing and were confident they had been careful.

"Go home," Malcolm suggested, "and come to the debriefing at 3 p.m. by the letterbox. By then we will have come up with either a result or a plan B."

A steady trickle of searchers reported back to us and went off home for lunch, saying they would be back. Then the pace slowed as those doing the difficult places took longer.

Malcolm, as I suspected he might, started talking about the Applebys.

"I'm going to have to determine whether Mr and Mrs Appleby have disappeared, whether they have shot through of their own volition, or perhaps come unstuck in some accident. Then, I suppose, we have to decide if someone could have done them in. They certainly seem to have enough enemies. We've had complaints about them for years."

"What sort of complaints?" I was unsure if I really wanted to hear the answer.

"This is a tad difficult for us. If I were to be open with you in confidence, I'd have to say I suspect the worst. These people aren't here, I reckon. All the signs point to their not being found on the farm. We have to look to be sure but my instinct and the look of the homestead indicate to me they aren't here.

"We'll be checking bank accounts and sightings shortly. Soon we will have to contact their family."

He paused awhile, as if deciding how much he should confide in me. "Actually, there isn't much we haven't had complaints about. I've been at this station for ten years, and this couple has occupied far too much of my time. Mainly it's just been accusations, but the social welfare agencies have decreed that he's not allowed to employ young people on the farm. He used to, but we had too many complaints from boys' parents, so we suggested in the right ears that it wasn't such a crash-hot idea. He's always being reported for growing dope, though we haven't found any, haven't looked that hard either. He's a stroppy little bastard. Not that he'd scare anybody. He or they just make the life of everyone involved a misery. When I send down a constable to look into something, he rings me. When I won't bow down, he rings my boss in Wanganui. He's been to HQ in Wellington a dozen times. Even the bloody Minister of Police. Over bugger-all."

"We've sometimes described the Apples as professional victims," I commented.

"That's it in a nutshell. Everything that goes on is some complex Machiavellian plot to bring him down. Just so much crap, really, but because he gets so antsy and belligerent everyone has to take him seriously.

"Stock rustling's another one," he continued. "Why can't these jokers sort out for themselves who owns what? It seems he's pinching a few from each neighbour on a regular basis, but no one's keen to take him to court. He's such a slippery customer."

Our family had always been pleased we didn't actually share a boundary with the Applebys, as we had heard stories or rumours of missing stock from other neighbours for years.

"How does he get away with it?" I asked.

"It seems he targets new, unsuspecting stock agents. He shows them stock of his own and they agree on a price, after an unusual amount of haggling, from what I hear. But the stock that arrives at the purchaser's place is not the same stock. He substitutes others he's pinched!

"Same with the meat companies. The stock the drafter is shown is not the stock that's sent to the works. It's no use talking about earmarks, I understand, because they don't check them when they're killing stock."

"So how come haven't you charged him?" I asked, knowing the answer full well.

"Nobody will go the whole hog and stand up to the prick in court," Malcolm replied.

"I understand that. These communities are too small in so many ways."

Malcolm concurred. "It's just been a frustration for us. We have spoken to all the stock companies and independent agents on the QT, but every year he does it again. Of course he doesn't sell that great an amount of stock; his other income seems to keep him going."

I concentrated on looking straight ahead, waiting for him to continue.

"Once again we have no proof," Malcolm went on, "but it's rumoured he's been growing dope here for years. We've flown over on numerous occasions, to no avail. With our budgets being trimmed every year it's damn hard to keep looking. Both local helicopter operators have agreed to keep an eye out. Appleby owes them both money so it's not been a problem, but so far there's been no result."

I thought to myself that it would be interesting to see what our volunteers found.

"It's those bad debts I'd love to see tackled." Malcolm turned as another ATV could be heard approaching. "The little prick owes every tradesman in town money. You know how much trouble our town has surviving economically without that sort of shit."

I agreed and we stopped there as Jack and his passenger pulled up. The policewoman, Sharon Lysaght.

"See anybody?" I asked as they turned the motor off.

"Not a soul," she replied, "but we found something interesting."

"There's a solar unit hooked up to a fence over there." Jack indicated where they had come from. "But the electric fence unit is just a blind; it's not actually doing anything. The solar panel is really powering something else."

On our farm at home we have a couple of solar units coupled to electric fence units to power new fences or beef up old fences. When you run an electric wire down one or sometimes both sides of an old but not-stuffed fence you stop animals poking their heads through to reach the sweeter grass on the other side. This gives the older fence an added life span and more importantly, keeps the bulls apart and stops goats wrecking the fences.

Jack was pleased with their discovery. "It's a far bigger unit than our larger one, more like a massive battery charger. There's a wire leading away from it underground. The trouble is, we can't tell where it goes to."

Malcolm asked a couple of questions about how far away it was and how easily accessible. "Only ten minutes ride from here and it's about 50 metres off the track."

X

After checking that we had enough time to get there and be back by our 3 p.m. deadline, Jack led the way with us on his tail to see what he had found. It didn't take long, and it was obviously a well used track to a part of the farm that didn't look to carry much stock.

We came to a small valley running west of the main dividing valley. A short way up this side shoot was a clearing about the size of a football field, facing north, and against one edge of the clearing the solar unit, with the lead-out wire running up and over the ridge and behind us down to the main track. Further left of the unit was scrub and regrowth bush. Ponga, ferns, mahoe, and makomako — it was usually a pleasure to see the distinctive crimson underside of their tooth-edged leaves in a breeze, and their clusters of wine-red berries. This, however, was not the time for a nature appreciation walk.

We all made our way up and around, and saw immediately that the solar unit was not powering the fence connected to its upright pole. The fence was buggered, whereas the unit was well cared for and high-powered.

The real cable led from the unit, went down the pole and under the bogus electric fence controller, not unlike a proper earth wire. A cursory look would have picked up nothing wrong, so I was impressed by Jack and Sharon's acuity.

We explained the workings of this type of unit to the police. How much fence a unit of its size could reasonably power and how the fence beside us served no purpose. They saw our point, so we tried pulling up the cable as Jack had done, to see where it went. No joy. We would need tools.

"Telecom," I said.

"What do you mean?" Malcolm was puzzled by my succinct remark.

"Telecom, or whoever does their servicing now, have a gadget for following cables underground. I saw it years ago when there was a cable that needed finding on a track our digger was working on. It would save shitloads of digging if you could borrow it."

Malcolm nodded his approval. "Good plan. Let's look into this scrub while we're here." Walking further away from the clearing, he stooped under the outside ponga and led the way into the undergrowth. I brought up the rear, keeping up; it was hard not to be curious about what he might find.

Within fifteen metres he stopped and we looked down into a small creek. Uphill to our right the creek came through a few broken rocks. Malcolm clambered up to the rocks and stopped again, peering intently. Crowding behind him, we made out a partly concealed opening which cut into the hill behind the rocks. He stood still for a minute, looking all around, then carefully turned and said, "I've got a sneaking suspicion of what we're going to find here. Let's go back and stop messing up what could be an important crime scene. We'll need to come back with cameras and maybe torches — and I'm not sure if we shouldn't get a warrant to cover all eventualities."

We retraced our path to the solar unit and down to our transport. Jack and I were keen as hell to guess what he suspected he had found. Curiosity was bursting out of us, or me, as I can't speak for both of us.

"What do you reckon?" I asked as we rode back down towards the homestead.

"Dope, I'd say," Malcolm replied.

"We have been looking outside for years, so he's gone underground." It was obvious.

"Hang on," I said, "that solar unit wouldn't drive that many lights."

"Wouldn't have to," he replied. "Access light only, I'd say. Let's wait until we come back and have a proper look."

Leaving Jack, the policewoman and a few others, we shot home so Malcolm could use the phone. His authority was obvious as he got through to who he wanted and made a few requests.

We drove back to the Applebys' mailbox to meet the others at the designated time. They were all there and no people had been found. Nor any bodies.

"Find anything interesting?" asked Malcolm straight up.

One by one the crews reported what they'd found. No humans seen by any of them. No sign of recent activity, nothing unusual. Our boys, Jack, Campbell and Murray spoke of the stock they'd seen. There was nothing much and nothing flash — the sheep were skinny and daggy.

Constable Joe, who had been riding with Charlie Durham, spoke up. "We found six or seven carefully concealed cages. They were very cunningly placed; it would have been easy to miss them if we hadn't stumbled right on top of them. He was obviously into market gardening in a big way once. But Charlie here reckons they haven't been used for three or four years, by the size of the scrub growing around them."

"Yeah, manuka this thick growing through the netting." Charlie held up a thick, work-toughened finger.

Malcolm said he thought he knew why the cages hadn't been used. He thanked everyone for giving the police a hand. "Without your help this would have become a major police operation. I know the search hasn't shown up much, but it's proved what we suspected. The Applebys aren't here. Haven't been for some time. Thanks for your time, your four-wheelers, and your cheerful co-operation." He went on, "Some of us came across what we suspect is an underground dope-growing operation, but there will be nothing growing there at this time of the year. We'll be back tomorrow with some drug squad guys from Wanganui. And a detective or two in case there's anything else there.

"Thanks again; I'll keep you informed of what's going on."

As the group started talking amongst themselves, he took Charlie Durham and me aside and asked if we could provide transport to take the police back to the solar panel tomorrow.

I said we could and Charlie agreed, so we left it there. Malcolm would ring tonight when a time for tomorrow was confirmed. Time to go home.

When I got there I went straight inside to describe our day to Georgina, who I knew would be hanging out to know what had happened. The boys did the dogs, ran the pups and came over as well to talk over the day and plan tomorrow's work.

First we shared what we had learned about the general run of the Appleby farm. We had all, especially the boys, seen more in the last two days than ever before.

Murray was first to speak. "How come, even though those people have been there for years, there's so little sign of any work been done?" He was right — you would have expected to see scrub cut, ring fern sprayed or burnt, fences in stockproof condition.

I watched and listened. Campbell replied that he thought they were idle bastards and Georgina, while not exactly coming to the Applebys' defence, asked what did we expect from such an odd couple.

"Yeah," Campbell agreed, "it's years since that last young one left, I suppose."

"There are bugger-all decent trees left in their bush," Jack cut in. We all looked at him.

"What do you mean?" Georgina looked puzzled for a moment.

"There are tracks all through their standing bush, made in the last few years, but there are only the stumps of big trees and just small trees left standing," Jack continued. "There's heaps of young beech, tawa, rewarewa — honeysuckle — and the like. You know, under-scrub, mahoe, five-finger, ponga, but all the big trees have gone."

"What was there?" I asked.

"I didn't stop to look, but I'd like to mooch back and find out," Jack replied. "We just rode past today. If I had an excuse I'd love to look again."

This wasn't our business, or part of our brief in helping the police, but strange nonetheless. Applebys had been known to rave about the enormous stands of kahikatea on the lower parts of their farm and huge rimu in the bush higher up, and other locals were envious. Our own bush had been cut ninety years ago, so any remnants in the valley were well worth saving.

"Would they have had resource consent to log it?" I wondered aloud.

"Most unlikely," Campbell replied. "The guys I know who have tried to get one since I've been home have had no joy at all."

After a while the boys went home, giving us some time for a glass of wine before dinner. Georgina was a little envious of our interesting day so I did my best to fill her in on any remaining details, such as my conversation with Malcolm. And there was still more to tell her about who had come to help search, what we had found, the lie of the land, and lastly Jack's observation about the bush being logged over.

With what the community had discovered today there would be heaps to chat about for months.

XI

The next day Malcolm returned with a bright young detective from Wanganui, Colin Smith. My latest rumination about the troubles of growing older was that people in authority were getting younger and younger.

We met Charlie Durham at the Applebys' gate and took two bikes onto their farm. Looking again at everything and anything for signs as we went. The hillsides were often covered in swaths of ring fern, with young manuka poking their heads through, and in the valleys glades of foxgloves competed with thistles for open ground and no doubt a cheery show of colour in season. Grazing was only available in the small patches of grass yet to be swallowed up by the encroaching scrub. Crown ferns and ponga were lining up to take over next. I described to Colin the layout of the place, stopping now and then to point out anything of interest. I told him who went where yesterday and answered a few general questions about Applebys' farming practices.

Talking about neighbouring farmers can be a sensitive subject to broach. We all operate a little differently and none of us is perfect, and who's to say who's right? But while we were not on this farm to judge the farmers, even a layman like Colin could see the place was run down. The easy country was covered in fern and foxgloves, a sign that no fertiliser had been applied for years. Weeds thrive in poor land; healthy grass would have stopped them regenerating.

We all, but especially Charlie and myself, agreed we still felt like trespassers traipsing around a farm we had never been welcome on. Charlie was concerned about what Appleby would say to him if they arrived back and found him there. I chipped in that I was worried too because I didn't want to get into a fight, but thought quietly to myself that actually I would have been very surprised indeed.

We arrived at last at the solar panel. Today we were transport only so Charlie and I parked the vehicles and watched the police push into the undergrowth. They hadn't yet arranged for Telecom's cable detector.

Charlie started talking as soon as the police were out of sight. He too had noticed the absence of big trees in the bush yesterday and was quite worked up about it.

"Ya know," he started, "these Regional Council types won't give me a consent to log anything on the back of our place, yet this bastard has taken every valuable tree and sold it."

"Where's the mill site?" I asked. Charlie had no idea, so we decided to ask the other locals who had been on the search yesterday if they had seen signs of one.

Charlie concentrated his gaze for a while on the smoke rings he was blowing, then flung a stone at a passing butterfly. "He must have pulled the logs and got some cowboy with a portable mill to saw the timber, then he must have carted it out at night. Otherwise we would all have seen something."

"Someone must have known something," I replied. "If you're really concerned, ask a few people up the road. He couldn't have gone past our places, but he had to pass farms further out the valley."

I paused for breath, and tried to take the steam out of the moment. "But what's the point of pursuing the illegal logging if the culprits have cleared off?" I knew full well that there could be no recriminations, because they were hardly going to reappear.

Charlie agreed, though it clearly did his temper no good to see someone getting away with something he himself wasn't allowed to.

"Waste of bloody time." He lit another smoke. "All the timber in the district wouldn't make this place profitable again." He was not far wrong there, but I couldn't see why he was still concerned.

Breaking in bush to create pasture a hundred years and more ago was how the pioneers made New Zealand what it is today. In hindsight, though, we cut ten percent too much bush, mainly on marginal, steep country. Any remnants cut now wouldn't make enough difference to an already shaky operation. Or, when all the timber had gone, the farm — and this one proved our theory — was just as bad, but now without trees. There are some people who just wouldn't learn.

Using the back of my bike as a table, we set out some sandwiches and leftover bacon-and-egg pie I'd brought for smoko, and we were just on our second cup of tea when the police arrived back.

"Not much of a find really," Colin reported as I passed him a cup.

"Great idea, no idea as well. The solar panel just powers the light leading the way in. Then there's a small hydroponics system, and a lighting set-up driven by a generator. Could have killed them."

"How so?" Charlie leaned forward.

"No ventilation. They may have had a fan but there's none there now. The carbon monoxide in there would have been dreadful."

"So our idea of a major drugs bust was a mite premature," Malcolm conceded.

"You made the right moves," Colin replied. "It had potential to be major, but the growers' plan wasn't followed up with the necessary practical expertise."

He couldn't organise a piss-up in a brewery, Jack had muttered yesterday. He was right enough about the horticultural enterprise; if only Appleby had been equally incapable of organising the plunder of the forest.

"There's nothing growing there now," Colin said. "It could have killed them. Cunning scheme, running water, secure from prying eyes, just no ventilation, or none that we could see."

We headed home, taking as much of a different path as we reasonably could. The police were still looking for live people, but we could tell that they were convinced the Applebys weren't here.

XII

Spring. Which is usually warming weather, but invariably damp. The ground underfoot is often slippery and mud sticks to boot and tyre treads, making walking and riding more dangerous than usual. The bush comes more alive in spring, with its chorus of birdsong early morning and often at dusk. This cut-over bush and scrub country has some of the forest birds of old, but fewer in number. There's always plenty of fantails darting around on the margins of the bush, and kereru and tui deeper within. In open farmland it's more common to see foreigners such as swallows, magpies and starlings, but the fantails are there too, and kahu the harrier gliding in search of mice, frogs, rabbits and other game, or dead stock.

Georgina had a large pot of pumpkin soup simmering when we got back home, so we had lunch and discussed where to next. Or the police did. Charlie's wife was in town so instead of going home he joined us too and we relaxed and listened to the police discuss how they planned to carry on the investigation.

Colin said he knew nothing of the legal process that must ensue.

Malcolm leaned back in his chair and scratched his head. "I'm not surprised you don't know. I've been a provincial cop for ten years, yet I've never heard of a place being abandoned before. That's what used to happen in the old days, in the Depression, but not for fifty years. I don't imagine there's going to be much of a protocol, a procedure to follow. We'll have to make inquiries with our legal people and go from there."

I listened to their conjecture and didn't add much as I couldn't think of a precedent either. I knew things like probate existed, but knew little of their purpose or reason.

Charlie was still bloody annoyed about the trees and wasn't really interested in who owned the farm if the Applebys didn't turn up.

Georgina, who had just been listening as well, asked whether anyone had searched the house.

Colin looked at Malcolm. "We just looked through all the windows on our first day out here. Best we go back and have a proper look."

Some of us were surprised that hadn't been done earlier, but thought better of saying anything.

Malcolm sensed our feelings. "You have to remember our history with these people. If they caught us snooping around their home without a warrant and a damn good excuse, my life wouldn't be worth living."

"Fair enough," said Colin, "but we'd better go and have another look. Sheds too, I expect."

"Can I use your phone?" He looked at me.

"Go for it." He took the cordless and wandered out to the verandah.

We finished second cups of tea and talked of nothing of consequence for five minutes while Colin made calls outside.

He came back inside looking business-like and thanked Georgina for lunch. "I've spoken to the Regional Commander, and he's given us the go-ahead to search everything we need to; he'll fax a warrant through. We'll go back and give the house and surrounds a thorough going-over now. Would you chaps like to have a look around the buildings and woolshed with us? Being farmers, you may notice things out of place that we wouldn't."

Charlie and I looked at each other briefly. "It feels strange poking around their place," Charlie said, "but so long as we're with you there shouldn't be any problems."

Colin mentioned that he had set legal inquiries in motion to see what the next move could be, and we went outside. Boots back on, we drove in convoy up the road to the Appleby house. For once they drove slowly because the road was slippery after early morning rain.

The policemen must have decided what they were going to do while they were on the road, and as soon as we arrived Colin went straight to the house front door while Malcolm led us in the opposite direction towards the old woolshed.

Our own woolshed was at least ninety years old but it held together and though it had been planned in another era it still functioned satisfactorily and wasn't worth replacing. This one of the Applebys looked rickety from a distance and in need of paint. From up close it was a miracle, a miracle that it was standing. There didn't look to be a sheep-proof pen in it. Baling twine seemed to be holding everything together. Walking through the yards to the shed was a risky business. You couldn't climb over the rails. They were unsafe, and the worn-out gateways, water-filled, all had baling twine-tied gates in various stages of disrepair across them.

We made the landing where wool was loaded onto trucks, and Charlie muttered to himself, as much as Malcolm and me, to be careful and watch where we walked. The steps had only half their treads still in place, and the landing deck itself sagged from rot and broken boards. The sliding door had been derailed, so Charlie and I took its weight between us and eased it open.

Inside was little different. Fadges — that's partly full wool bales — lay strewn haphazardly against the walls, oddments of dags and wool littered the floor, skins hanging over many rails around the catching pens. Killing obviously took place here, as a gambrel hung above the first pen, although there was no blood or other sign that any carcass had hung from it in recent weeks. Some of the skins were wizened and tatty and had clearly been hanging on the rails for months, chewed by rats or mice.

The wool press was an early model, Noah's maybe, and the top box was lifted up by a block-and-tackle arrangement slung from a rough-sawn rimu four-by-two rafter. Any government or council building inspectors would have run out of infringement notices and declared the place unfit within minutes. Again green baling twine featured predominantly in the construction, or lack of it. There was an old work bench along one wall, but you couldn't actually work at it. It was piled high with old fencing tools, assorted boxes, smoko gear and junk. Some of the gear hanging around the walls was from a long distant past. Old scythes, slash hooks, and antique horse harness gear such as swingle trees I vaguely recognised as we looked about. Instead of pillaging his bush, Appleby should have carted the lot off to a junk shop, he would have certainly made a bob or two.

Malcolm called out from the end of the three-stand shearing board. "There's a deep water trough thing out here."

Charlie and I walked along the board. The three shearing machines were electric, rather than the old shafting plant of yesteryear, were three different models, and were nailed up to the wall. An electric shearing machine should be sited on a beam high on the wall of a shearing shed opposite the catching pens and in front of the counting pens. From it hangs a movable dropper with a spinning shaft inside. From the bottom of the dropper is an elbow with a short shaft, half a metre, connecting to the handpiece, not unlike the clippers a barber uses, which actually shears the wool. All this gear is usually bolted onto a twelve-by-four beam, so that it doesn't all fall down onto the shearers' heads. Nailing such heavy equipment up was unbelievably bloody stupid, and it was hard to imagine contract shearers would have been prepared to work in such conditions. Perhaps Appleby did the deed himself.

Out where a window had once been was an old plunge sheep dip, the sort where the sheep had been run along a race onto a board sloped at 50 or 60 degrees, from which they fell into a long dip. Once in, they had to swim six or seven metres through the dip to where they could climb out into a concrete draining pen.

The farmer would use a special tool to push the sheep's heads under as they swam, and could fish them up if they stayed under too long. The whole thing hadn't seen a sheep for years and wouldn't hold a sheep now if you wanted it to. But the dip was full of water.

"We'll have to drain that," Malcolm said. Charlie, who knew more about these things than I did, went around the back of the third catching pen and swung down to the ground. Shortly we could hear water running and then gushing out as he had opened up a drainage system.

It only took five minutes as Malcolm, Charlie and I watched. The two of them leaned in closer as the water dropped, and I peered with them as if I had no idea what we'd find. Again, no bodies. The relief on Charlie's face was obvious.

Nearby was an old water tank also made of concrete, but we could all see at a glance it held no bodies either, let alone water — you could peer in through the cracks.

We continued out through the forcing pens to the holding area at the back. The wooden grating out here was lower than the front and was in fact sitting on the ground. The piles had long since rotted off at ground level and the floor of the shed had settled onto the mud and dirt.

Through the back door to the drafting yards there was evidence of the same lack of maintenance and the inevitable catalogue of deterioration. The drafting race was so worn down it was full of water. It would need work before a sheep would run through it willingly.

We passed the yards and looked over the back towards the river. There was a few years' accumulation of rubbish thrown over the bank here, some of which would have found its way to the river. Charming. The pile was partially covered in pig fern and blackberry, and wouldn't have been visible from the road.

Malcolm led the way from this old dump over to the car shed. He prised the half-door apart and squeezed through, to behind, then alongside the car. He peered in, then opened the driver's door, looking in and around.

Bees had made a hive in the rafters above the engine, but the hive looked quiet, so I said nothing. Coming back out we gave the old ATV a cursory look, taking care not to put pawprints on anything, and wandered back towards the house.

Colin was waiting for us and obviously hadn't found anything either.

"It just looks as though they walked away and didn't return," he said. "Everything looks absolutely normal. Dishes in the sink, reasonably fresh food in the fridge and cupboards. A few beds made up but not slept in recently. The house is just abandoned. Christ knows what's happened to them."

His search so far had not turned up the Applebys' passports, but Coin said that was inconclusive as they could have them safely stored somewhere. It would be easy to see if they had been used at any port or airport.

The whole place had a depressing air about it. Neglect. The actual site wasn't bad. Well sheltered by a stand of rimu on one side. Not forest giant rimu, but 30 to 50-year-old juveniles, their long spiky leaves flowing down in graceful branches to make their distinctive conical shape. The remains of a decent hydrangea-fringed garden surrounded the rest of the house, but a lawnmower hadn't been used here for some time. Sheep had been coming in through the broken front gate to mow the grass, and while there had pruned most of the trees up as high as they could reach. Around the front with a glimpse of the river was an old verandah, where sheep had also camped and left their calling cards beneath the bedroom windows. Delightful.

There were chooks as well, but it was a long while since they had been locked in. Their enclosure door was lying in the grass, and their fence sagged low with vines growing over it.

We all walked around the section, nosing and prodding, and ended back at our vehicles.

Charlie is one of these laconic characters who particularly avoids saying much in the way of commenting on people, and certainly doesn't diss them. You could tell though that he was disgusted with what he had just seen. He brooded, hands deep in his pockets and his head down. You could hear him thinking what useless bastards we were dealing with.

Colin was unsure what to do next and even Malcolm looked a little perplexed.

They thanked us for our help and after chat about this and that we left them to their work.

Charlie and I didn't speak until I pulled up at his back gate and switched off the motor. "I could do with a spot after that," he said. "Like to join me?" We walked up the path and he opened the door, then he stopped and lit a smoke.

XIII

Charlie's place wasn't pristine in a city sort of way, but it was neat and obviously very productive. From the gate to the porch winter vegetables grew in neat rows and the ground was already laboriously dug over in preparation for spring planting.

The back porch was rife with boots, coats, hats and umbrellas. The kitchen had an old Rayburn woodstove ticking over to keep the chill off, banked up with solid hunks of kanuka.

In practised movements Charlie went to the sideboard and gathered two glasses in one hand and a jug and bottle of Scotch in the other. Putting the glasses down near me, he invited me to do the honours and went to put water in the jug. Spring water. Similar to ours and a perfect complement to whisky.

I poured half an inch in each glass and Charlie poured an equal amount of water on top. One of the many things I admire about Charlie is his taste in whisky. Glenlivet — one of the best. Pigeon's milk. We toasted each other's health and settled down for a yarn.

"You know, Tony," he started, "it's years since I've been over to the Applebys', and not for want of trying." To be neighbourly, he meant. Georgina had done her best too, offering invitations to gardening circle activities and other local gatherings in the early days.

"Yeah, I think I know how you feel, but it takes all types," I replied noncommittally.

"Not really," Charlie said. "I mean, it takes all types, sure, but some types are too much trouble. Those people are takers. They have raped that place. It wasn't that flash when they went there, but it's only leapt backwards since."

I was gearing up to change the conversation's course a little. Charlie wanted to wind into them I could tell, and while he had every right, I wanted a little information.

"I agree, Charlie. None of us knows what happened there, but looking at the state of the place it's only a matter of time before they are forced off because the farm wouldn't be paying its way. Do you know where the kids are?" Meaning the Appleby kids.

Charlie thought for a few seconds before replying. "I haven't heard for ages. Last I knew, one was in Aussie, the older boy I think. One was up north somewhere and the daughter — no idea."

Up north to Charlie meant anything from north of Taumarunui, possibly as far as Cape Reinga.

But he wasn't to be distracted either and he looked at me seriously. He knows of my small interest in things political. He knew of our family's stand on sustainable farming methods and the need for conservation.

"For five years now I've wanted to pull a couple of rimu out of our back country. The wife wants a trip overseas, and she wants the kitchen done up. The farm pays its way okay, but only just. Not much surplus, no margin for error. Just two or three rimu is all I want. Will the Council let me? Not on your nelly. It has to be done sustainably, fair enough. But I've been asking for three years now and have got nowhere going through the proper channels. I nip next door with you to search for my neighbours and they've taken a hundred rimu. Maybe hundreds, Christ knows. And I have no idea how many kahikatea. I can't bear to think."

He was talking about the kahikatea, and he told me more

in those few sentences than I'd ever heard from him before. Sure his farm was smaller than ours, but he'd been here a lot longer. To hear how marginal it was came as a revelation to me. And a couple of rimu out of however many dozen he had would make a substantial difference to him and his wife. I sympathised. But Charlie was a by-the-book man and wouldn't willingly buck the system. To him, the fact that the Applebys had logged lots of bush meant a rank injustice. Going by the book, he couldn't get permission to mill even two trees.

The Applebys' surreptitious flouting of the regulations may have seen a hundred hectares of native bush logged over. And whoever was meant to enforce the Resource Management Act, or Forest Amendment Act, had let them get away with it. To say Charlie was gutted by this situation would be an understatement.

Charlie also knew that one whisky on its own was never enough, so he slid his empty glass in my direction. Three, I also knew, was his limit. Not normally an emotional chap, he was stirred up. He reached for his smokes and offered me one. Reformed smoker and strong-willed as I am, I took one. Charlie wasn't really supposed to smoke in the kitchen so he grabbed an ashtray from the porch and left the door open as a compromise.

"What about the stock?" I asked him. "The ewes, hoggets and both sexes mixed together. Should we do something?"

Charlie stared at his glass and didn't respond immediately, so I continued. "Our system at home is obviously a shade more complicated than the Applebys', but shouldn't we draft off the ewes so they can lamb separately?"

Charlie interrupted with language not normally heard in the kitchen. "Fuck them!"

I knew where he was coming from and didn't disagree, so I didn't push it. I knew the boys at home were keen to see something done, though, possibly more out of curiosity than benevolence.

We passed the bottle once more, nattering and smoking together until it was time for me to push off home. It was dark now, but only six o'clock, and I drove slowly home, my mind busy with a thousand thoughts. Firstly sympathy for the Durhams' situation, not that it was serious, but they needed a break in their fortunes. And my mind was circling back uncertainly to the situation I had helped create or at least exacerbate. What about the cost and time of all the searching for neighbours who I knew perfectly well weren't there?

XIV

The boys were all away working stock: ensuring that the ewes were spread out and not hanging round the gateways, checking that the lambing hadn't started. Georgina was in town for supplies. Well, we say we have to go out for supplies but there's no doubt it would be more efficient to go out once every few months and bring a great stack of necessaries home in a truckload. We could just as easily store ten sacks of flour as a 5-kilo bag, but it's a reality check to get out of the valley once a week or so. Some rural people who don't get out enough become more than a little introverted, to put it politely. We like to wander up and down the main street saying gidday to a few acquaintances, shopkeepers and the like, before heading back up the valley — realising with every mile travelled closer to home, how lucky we are to live there. No doubt Georgina would be combining the trip with a quilters' meeting, with probably a visit to the accountant thrown in. I knew which she would enjoy more.

I decided to take a little time out and get my thoughts into some sort of order. The session at Charlie's had started me thinking, but I didn't know where my thoughts were leading me. Going to the boot cupboard, I picked a well-worn pair of hobnails, with tricounis on the sides for better grip, and tied them on tight. Then went to the kennels and collected Lizard, Beck and Ned. The latter two are huntaways and they prance around for a while barking at everything, but after a few minutes they settle down and come in behind. I set off north, climbing for the first kilometre on a road cut deep into the slope of the hill. Then the farm opens up and the track levels out. Opens up into a picturesque valley with the Makakote Stream at the bottom. On the right is a hill running to steep bluff on top, and on the left the hill evens out to a long narrow flat beside the creek. Beyond the creek the hills rise to the west side of the home valley, again to bluff on top, with some fertile land between creek and cliff.

In my own mind I wanted to make sure that I wasn't painting myself into a corner with this Appleby business. Strangely, maybe, I didn't seem to have big feelings of guilt for keeping quiet about what I knew, or for knowingly wasting everybody's time. It seemed more like I was letting nature take its course. I hoped this wasn't just a rationalisation.

Years ago I'd learnt the value of biding my time. When we were young and fit and working flat out it was often easier to let an unsuitable employee find out for himself that he'd chosen the wrong career in farming. Let him decide that hard work wasn't for him, that early mornings and long wet days weren't really that much fun. Rather than take the more direct route, calling him a useless prick and saying that if he didn't shoot through soon I'd kick his arse until he did.

Much less pain all around to wait for him to resolve the discomfort himself, and the situation would sort itself out.

During the time that had passed since the Applebys disappeared, the things that had happened seemed in my mind to have been a natural progression. If allowed to follow their own course the matter would eventually end up quietly resolved, and the world would be a better place without them polluting it.

I've always been something of a worrier, so my family tell me, but I prefer to think of it as covering all the likely outcomes before they occur. The old 'time spent in reconnaissance is seldom wasted' theory. Must have got it from my father, whose main job in the desert war was reconnoitering behind enemy lines, keeping an eye on enemy troops, making a few pre-emptive strikes, and scouting out paths that would make the allied forces' battle plans and escape routes more effective. Rather than charging into action like a bull at a gate, and then wondering why the outcomes didn't match the ambitions.

Georgina's and my progress through agricultural contracting to farming, then acquiring successively bigger and bigger farms has been a slow, methodical process. Of waiting for capital gain to make debt look smaller before raising the eyes — and the sights — to look at the next opportunity. Compared to strategic plans, leverage of debt, taking uncalculated risks.

With the Appleby business I'd stepped outside fifty years of experience and taken a course quite alien to any previous philosophy. Quite unlike me. Yet all the time it had seemed like the logical thing to do. The purpose of my walk now was to clear my mind, go over what had happened, ponder what twists and turns could ensue, and what likely fallout could result.

So I wandered north. One hour, then two, reaching the top yards and the nearby hut around 11 a.m. The top hut has always been stocked with a few provisions, so that if any of us were caught out by the weather, or if a job at the yards stretched longer than planned, there were the makings of tea or coffee, a jar of snacks — chocolate bars and the like — often raided, I'd have to add. I sat on the step to rest my bones and look over the back paddocks.

Liz decided there was a possum up a mahoe below the hut, and the huntaways showed a little interest for a while, then they sat down near me and left Liz to be staunch alone.

From here I could look over our back country, some of Charlie Durham's flats and beyond to the Applebys'. Not much of theirs but enough to see the colour of grass, scrub cover and patches of bush. Possibly a couple of hundred hectares, a third of their farm.

I started thinking about their stock. Where we were up to in our farm's spring programme must have some similarities to theirs. There would be quite a stack of work to do for the stock's health when someone decided to take charge. Or until someone turned up.

We don't love our sheep in the Australian sense, but it's a waste of time farming animals you don't like or respect.

Liz brought me back from my thoughts by starting to bark, so I hopped over the nine-wire fence and found a stick. Longer than my walking pole, long enough to poke into the mahoe she was underneath.

I soon located the possum and knocked it down to reward Liz for her great skill, which she clearly felt. She quickly dispatched the possum and carried it back to Ned and Beck, no doubt to show her hunting prowess and colossal intellect. They all fell in behind as I clambered back onto the track and set off again for home. Liz soon tired of carrying her prize and stowed it in a rata log for lunch another day. Then she rolled over and over in the grass in some inscrutable dog ritual, and rejoined us looking very superior.

The walk home was generally downhill and different in aspect. Cruising along towards lunch. The boys passed on the lower track, towing dogs on small trailers behind their ATVs, and to a questioning yell I waved them on.

My mind was at ease. Nothing that had happened seemed to have left any dark worries at either the centre or the periphery of my mind. There was no suggestion of that lurking feeling that you have forgotten something, nor any intimation of impending doom. Such as the feelings that used to precede meetings with bank managers over the annual budget and cashflow in earlier development years.

Rightly or wrongly I felt scarcely a glimmer of guilt, so

couldn't see any reason not to just sit back and see what eventuated. While I'd hitherto kept no secrets from my family, I was surprised to find that I felt no guilt withholding from them the information I had acquired. The search for ghosts on the Appleby farm at least had the benefit of giving the boys the chance to look over a piece of land they'd been fascinated by for ages, and was just part of the huge adventure of living and working in this part of country. For Georgina the events were an interesting diversion, but neither upsetting nor worrying. Her social responsibility side was in gear out of typical concern for others, and it wasn't interfering with her other current major preoccupation, planning a surprise party for Murray before he departed. Why burden any of them with the confidentiality I had offered to young Brent and Jan Appleby? It was hard enough for me playing dumb, and telling more people only increased the risk that the favour Brent had done the world would turn sour and stuff up even more lives.

The police I'd met during the searches seemed to be bright, open-minded characters, well aware of the dubious idiosyncracies of the missing couple. Yet also mindful of the need of the need to reach some sort of closure on the case.

Appleby had been described to me as a vexatious litigant by the detective Colin Smith, and while the words took a bit of working out, it seemed to me the police had the measure of the man. Naturally they would want to see justice done. But as yet there was no apparent injustice. So life would go on. What would be would be; I found myself whistling *'Que sera sera'* as I opened the last gate into the home paddock. What will be, will be.

XV

I locked up the dogs, collected the mail and made my way inside. After a quick scan of the numerous envelopes for anything interesting I put the jug on and settled down with the *Herald*. One of life's small, under-appreciated pleasures. Reading the daily paper.

No sooner had I turned to the sports page than I heard an unfamiliar vehicle pulling up in the carpark. Looking out, I saw there was a white ute with two guys hopping out. A short fat one and a tall thin one, they wandered over to Campbell's house, so I continued reading. But my enjoyment was gone. I got up to see whose ute it was, and from the kitchen window I could see the local bureaucrats' livery and bold slogan: "Regional Council – *Out there working*."

They soon turned in the direction of our house, so I sat down and awaited their arrival. Campbell with them.

"These guys from the Regional Council have come to ask about the Applebys," Campbell started. The two blokes came inside and I recognised the vertically challenged one as a regular, Rodney Buckland, who had been around for yonks. They came in and sat around the table. I folded my paper.

"We've heard through the grapevine," Buckland started, "that you have been through the Applebys' place lately."

"A whole heap of us have," I replied. "We've been helping the police try to find them. They've been missing for a while now." As though anybody within a hundred kilometres wouldn't know.

"What we've actually heard," Buckland homed in on the point of his visit, "is that he has illegally logged all his native bush."

"So what's that to do with us?" Campbell asked politely, but he wasn't being polite.

"Nothing directly," replied Buckland. "We're just looking for info re their use of their resource consent."

"Why don't you go and have a look yourselves?" Campbell asked. "We don't even share a boundary with their place. Had no idea they were logging, for that matter."

I was becoming interested. Firstly I couldn't work out why they were here. If the Applebys had a consent, surely it was a matter between them and the Regional Council. As politely as I could manage I asked Rodney, "What's the story here? If they have consent to log, go and see what's happening. As Campbell says, we have no idea what they get up to."

Rodney Buckland had the decency to look sheepish. "Well, actually he doesn't have a logging consent. He has a consent to put in a tourist road, so they can show people through their virgin bush. But we've heard a rumour they haven't respected that consent."

"So have a look. What's the problem?" I repeated.

"Not that simple," Bruce replied. "He's denied access in the past. Some stuff about his access bridge and the occupational safety and health legislation. He wants us to sign a disclaimer of responsibility before he will allow us in. Crap really, but he's been so bellicose, we haven't been able to pursue it."

Campbell snorted. "You mean to tell me that you haven't bothered to have a look at what he's up to because you're scared of the little prick?"

Bucko looked at his offsider, still unintroduced, then looked down at his hands before replying. "Not so much scared. If we argue with him, he just gives my boss heaps, and so on up the chain of command." A similar story to the one the police had told.

"So? He's missing," observed Campbell. "Go in and have a look, there's no one there. Between all of us in the valley there's been hundreds of hours looking, and there are no Applebys at home."

Bucko appeared to be unsure, unconvinced. Campbell, I could tell, was disgusted. I wasn't sure where we fitted in. Why they were here? Then it dawned on Campbell and me at around the same time.

"You want us to take you through their farm, don't you?" challenged Campbell. Disbelieving.

"All your powers and all your staff, all your resources, you want us to take you in!"

That is exactly what they wanted of us and Campbell was not a happy chap. But my curiosity had moved from mild interest and was peaking at fascination. Sure, I privately agreed with Campbell. These were gutless men. Career civil servants. But I also had this innate curiosity, now on red alert. I hadn't actually seen that much of the Appleby farm in the searches. And certainly little of their bush. Our own farm was largely bereft of native bush. The early settlers, the farm's first owners, slashed and burned everything in their path. All around us there was National Park with virgin native bush but on our own farm, only our own plantings were redressing the balance.

There was another interest as well — livestock. Their sheep. What was going to happen to them? I didn't mention this aspect, as it was none of their business. But I asked, "Transport, what have you guys got?"

"We have a 4 x 4 ATV on a trailer back up at the Applebys' gateway."

"Okay," I said, "let's go." They had ruined my lunchtime ritual, so some interesting benefit had better come of it.

The regional guys went to their ute. We agreed to meet at the Applebys' gateway in twenty minutes and they drove off.

"What do you reckon?" Campbell asked, surprised I think by my response, but I knew that there was very little chance of us being caught in the act by the Applebys on their return. I could pretty much guarantee a no-show as far as they were concerned.

Not that I was going to say that. "Look," I said, "on one hand I'm very reluctant to get involved. But on the other there are two things. Firstly, I'll admit I'm bloody keen to see what's been going on over there. Secondly, someone's going to have to make some decisions soon."

"What sort of decisions do you mean?" Campbell asked.

"Simple, really. No one's doing anything or said anything about their stock. No matter what has happened, someone has to take charge until an Appleby or someone who is their executor turns up to take a look."

Campbell agreed straight away. We hadn't been on the same wavelength.

"Ring Jack," I said. "Tell him what we're up to. I'll ring Charlie Durham. See if he wants to come with us. Covering my back."

XVI

Charlie wasn't home. He had short lunches. I left a message on his answerphone about our plans and said I'd talk to him tonight. Then got my warmer riding gear on and met Campbell at the shed. We took one ATV, Campbell riding and me sitting on the side, and buzzed off up the road. Rodney and his lanky mate were waiting, and without any further mucking about we proceeded towards the centre of the Applebys' farm. Close to my base with the police last time.

We stopped and asked Rodney where exactly he wanted to go. From inside his Swanndri he pulled out one of those plastic-wrapped topographical maps, on which was highlighted the area covered by resource consent. We were in the wrong place. The area covered was on the eastern side of the farm, so we set off in that direction.

Quite quickly the scrub ran out at a creek bottom. We crossed over a papa ford, rose into native bush and soon found ourselves at an old mill site, by the look of the slabs stacked around. And dumped into the creek. Bastards. There was no milling gear. Just slabs of beautiful kahikatea, the 'white pine' first made famous in the butter and cheese box days before the coming of cardboard, and rimu, now a high-class furniture timber. In the rare event that you could get it.

We scouted around and found a track to follow, obviously a logging track as it was scoured deep where trees had been dragged out by bulldozer. It soon became clear as we climbed up and east that there was a problem here. I'd seen cut-over bush before at Mamaku, north of Rotorua. And this was cut over. From a distance it had looked as if there were plenty of trees left, but down here, up close, all the big mothers were gone.

Regrowth had covered much of the damage that had been done to the forest. Ferns, supplejack and weeds sprang about in profusion, but the evidence was still there. Tawa trees smashed in half, pushed over. The saddest sights were remnant heads of rimu, skeleton-like amongst crushed ponga, all the rich red timber stripped and sawn, just the unmillable head branches left to rot. The occasional huge stump left after the trunk had been cut off above the buttress. We rode on in silence. Jack had been right. Without anyone knowing, all the reasonably accessible trees had been illegally logged.

Other trees remained. Stands of low-value tawa, no-value hinau. Vast patches of mamaku, ponga and other tree ferns. Hundreds of rewarewa, tall but spindly kahikatea ... a deathly absence of big rimu, except in gullies too steep even for the bulldozer. The high-value wood was all plundered.

We stopped again on a high saddle, where the right-hand track was blocked with the remains of a tawa, and the left fork partially obscured by a fallen mahoe. Turned the bikes off, and looked around at the poorly disguised devastation.

Rodney's mate finally made a contribution. He was quietly spoken and obviously intelligent, which became evident as he started to speak.

"This is terrible," he said. Rodney looked glum and dumb. "This is a bloody travesty. This consent is for a tourist road to show people the trees, but every time the road reaches a tree it's been cut down. Bloody hell." From his coat he pulled out a folder and spread its contents on the back of our bike. We stopped looking at the devastated bush and looked at the resource consent. Or I did. Picking it up. It had the same map we had seen before, and a written reason for the consent, a couple of pages of conditions. The reason was the tourist route and clearly defined. The conditions were another matter. I read them quickly: *no bulldozers, only digger work allowed, proper track formation, proper water management,* and *no unnecessary damage to occur to anything* had all been highlighted by a fluorescent pen. It only took a few seconds to realise that every consent condition had been violated. Totally. I passed the document to Campbell for his closer perusal and turned to the skinny bloke.

"What's your involvement here, chief?"

"Sorry, should have introduced myself. I'm Sean Whitworth," he replied. "I'm with the soil conservation side of the Regional Council."

I noticed two things. He was distancing himself from the Rodney Buckland bureaucratic type, and he was intimating to me he was a cut above with the benefit of a background in science.

"We set the conditions by which this consent was granted, which were meant to be adhered to, and which were meant to be policed," he continued. I glanced at Rodney, who looked as if he wanted to crawl under a log. I didn't know much about Regional Council systems, but if there was any justice in the world he was in deep doodoo.

There was no recent work here. To my eye, and judging by the regrowth, it was all a year or two old.

"How long has he had a consent, and how long is it for?" I inquired.

"We granted it three years ago," Sean replied, "and it's for fifteen years. But no more, it's been flagrantly abused."

It seemed to me that there was little he could do now. All the prize trees were gone and only time, eons of time, would rebuild the damage. Really, another forest had to grow here.

The giants that should have stood all around us were no

more. You could see some on a steeper ridge to the north, the usual line of beech along the eastern ridge running north-south. What remained, though, was not a tourist attraction. What was left was a mess of broken trees and regeneration. It wouldn't be worth bringing tourists up this track to see big trees for another five hundred years or so.

Rodney Buckland sat and stared at his hands. Sean Whitworth paced about quietly fuming and Campbell and I sat pondering the vicissitudes of life. I knew Rodney's mind would be in damage control mode, working out whether he could worm his way out of a situation in which he was clearly complicit. Buckland had to have known about the illegal logging but had done nothing about it. An easier option than challenging Appleby.

The controversial Resource Management Act is not really bad legislation. Its intent is honourable but its implementation has left much to be desired. Practically you can't argue about protecting the environment, but you could argue that getting rich at the resource applicant's expense is unjust. The cost of employing resource management consultants, paying consent objectors' fees, and Regional Council staff's hourly rates — all over $80 an hour — are all costs of doing business associated with the Resource Management Act or the Forest Amendment Act.

Equally, we all know that in the development of our agriculture-based economy we have cut down too much bush. Preserving what remains has to be a national priority. The singularly ironic aspect occurred to me at this point. We were inspecting, standing in, an uneconomic, badly farmed property. After logging all this virgin bush, the farm was still badly farmed and uneconomic. Ravaging the bush had achieved nothing tangible that I'd seen in my travels around the place, unless there was a bloated bank account stashed somewhere. That seemed unlikely.

To make matters worse, the Regional Council had let it happen, and anything they did now would be ineffectual. Suing dead people couldn't be that productive. Where to from here?

Sean returned looking quite woebegone after a brief foray up past the mahoe that was blocking bike access. He looked as though he didn't want a lot to do with his colleague, and approached us instead.

XVII

"Thanks for showing us this place," Sean started. "I'll come back geared up with a camera and make a proper report. Is there any chance Appleby will turn up?"

Campbell said that it didn't look likely. He told Sean some of what we had achieved with the police searches. That it seemed improbable that they were alive and yet there was no sign of them having cleared out.

"Who will take over?" Sean asked, and I replied that this was a question many were asking and as yet no one had told us anything.

"I'll talk to our in-house lawyer in Palmerston North," Sean said. "I think we can achieve nothing more here."

"We can, actually," I said. "We want to look at the livestock on the way out. Someone's going to have to make some decisions soon. Not us, but someone in authority is going to have to do something. Your man may know, or the police will have to use their discretion."

"How do you mean?" Sean asked.

"Well, there must be a thousand or so ewes here ready to lamb," I told him. "They need vaccinating, crutching and set stocking, although they seem to be permanently set-stocked. Just your usual pre-lambing management. Someone needs to do something."

"Rather you than me," said Sean. We turned around and started back. On this occasion though we took a roundabout route and, for the first time since this sorry saga began, we took a close look at the stock.

We rode slowly to have a good look. It wasn't that encouraging. There appeared to be a real hodgepodge of mixed-aged ewes. Scattered through them were a number of light, underfed woolly hoggets. At least the hoggets appeared not to be in lamb. They were too skinny to be pregnant, or even to get pregnant.

Campbell was passenger now. I was riding and looking, he was looking and counting. And though we had no mandate, nor any intention to make an accurate count, it could be handy to know roughly what was here.

There appeared to be few cattle, which simplified matters. We rode on, and after seeing more than half of the open country we had seen enough. There were around eight hundred sheep, of which seven hundred seemed to be ewes, the remainder hoggets and a few rams. Which appeared to be permanently with the ewes. Normally hoggets are farmed separately, on better country, so that they can grow to their full potential before being put out to the rams. Some hoggets are lambed, but only if they are over 40kg live weight at around eight months of age.

The few holding paddocks near the house and tumbled-down woolshed were open to the rest of the farm, and had no more grass than the rest. Campbell suggested we shut up a holding paddock or two, but I said taihoa — by and by — better wait until someone took charge. I had no intention of showing that our family wanted to take over the situation. We would help if asked, but remain in the rearguard of any action. Too often I'd seen small community initiatives blow back in the instigator's face. Even after being here twenty years we were still looked on by some as being outsiders. And because our farming methods were seen to be progressive, there was a backward element waiting to shoot us down. It didn't particularly worry me, it was just typical Kiwi local sensitivities and politics, the likes of which were to be found in most rural communities. At least we weren't on the West Coast of the South Island, where it could take two generations before a family was considered local.

We saw Charlie Durham out collecting his mail on the way back, and leaving the Regional Council guys to go on and load their bike, we rode over to him. After the normal pleasantries essential with Charlie we described what we had done. Charlie is a good joker. A friendly neighbour, a skilled stockman you could always usefully consult about animal health or diet. He had a few concerns about the welfare of the animals himself, so he was actually pleased that we, using the Regional Council as an excuse, had looked over the livestock. Charlie said he didn't know if the Applebys did much in the way of vaccinating sheep pre-lamb but would give us a hand if we decided to. I asked him what he thought the next move should be. He paused, lighting one of his tailor-mades, giving himself a little time to think.

"I reckon leave it to the police," he said at last. "Let them find who the executors are or whatever, then we can offer to help if approached."

"Suits us," I said, and after another round of talk about prospects for the weather and the state of the road we said our goodbyes. Back over to Rodney and Sean Regional Council. Rodney, much less the boss now, left the talking to Sean. "Thanks for your help, I'll do a report, come back for photos, and see what happens."

Same as all of us, I thought, and off they went.

We rode home and as you'd by now have come to expect, everyone there was fairly keen to hear what we had been up to. Around the table Campbell led off and I sat back listening to him describe the day's dramas, saying little until he was finished.

The family were united in their condemnation of what the Applebys had done to their bush, and several theories were presented as to how they had got away with it.

"Simply that all of us down this road have had so little to do with them," Georgina suggested, to general agreement.

"What will happen to the Regional Council guys?" Murray wanted to know.

"Nothing," I replied. "They look after their own, while they are meant to look after the RMA, when push comes to shove they really aren't that accountable."

We talked around the issues involved for a while, deciding to maybe ring the police tomorrow to see if there was any progress.

I settled down in my armchair to catch up with the sports news, realising I couldn't say anything, accepting quietly to myself that what would be, would be.

Georgina was as usual keen to hear of our efforts and discoveries and wasn't surprised about the condition of the place. She is much more able than I am to see the good side of people, but in this case even she was hard-pressed to find nice things to say.

XVIII

Ewes had started lambing at home, at least a few early ones. While we didn't need to do a formal lambing beat with our Perendale/Finn-Romney flock, bred as they were for easy care, with so many valuable ewes on the farm we rode around most of them every day. We had few birthing problems with our lambs but there were always a few ewes heavily in lamb who had sat down to chew or sleep, rolled into a small hollow, and had been unable to stand up again. After a few hours of being cast like this they often died — an awful death and a senseless waste, so we rode around to check.

Otherwise our winter maintenance programme ran on into spring, everyone being busy every fine day. We had started strip-grazing our cows before they calved, on mature pasture saved from last autumn's growth. This maintained their body weight while conserving feed so that their rations could be increased after calving. I enjoyed this routine every spring, except for the first few days when many of the cows that hadn't met with a single-wire electric fence since last calving did their best to beat the system and break out.

*

Coming home for lunch a week or so after our search of the Applebys' I knew by Georgina's demeanor that something was up, even before I went inside.

"There's a call coming for you at 12.30," she said. "Someone who wouldn't give me their name. I think it's something to do with up the road." Meaning Apples. I hoped to hell it wasn't going to be Brent ringing while Georgina was within earshot.

Normally if someone wouldn't give their name to my wife or do business with her we would cut them off and not have anything to do with them. If they came or rang and wanted to speak to me alone, they were given the bum's rush. Georgina and I had earned this farm together. There were people who didn't want to deal with her because she was female, and we had given quite a few of them a surprise over the years. But Georgina had guessed that this caller had other reasons for being evasive.

Sure enough, at 12.30ish the phone rang.

"Is that the Prices' place?" said the voice.

"Yes," I answered cautiously. "Tony Price speaking."

"Trevor Appleby here. I don't think we've met, but we used to live up the road from you. I'm trying to contact my parents, but either there's no reply or the phone's been cut off, you can't tell which. Do you know where they are?"

Trevor. I was immediately at a loss as what to tell him, or how much. Then I thought fast.

"We've been asked by the police to help look for your folks. They haven't been seen for the best part of a month now, and no one knows anything. For the official version, I'll give you the policeman's name, if you like."

He liked, so I gave him Malcolm's name, station and phone number. "We've been wondering," I said, "what to do with your father's sheep. They must be due to lamb, and there are things that should be done."

"I'd say it's none of your business," Appleby Junior replied with a breathtaking lack of tact. "I'll sort out whatever needs doing."

With that attitude and the fact that I'm normally rather short with rude people, I gently replaced the phone on its cradle on the wall, and sat down to tell Georgina that some of the family's less charming points had survived a generation.

Then I got up again to ring Charlie Durham and tell him of Trevor Appleby's call. Charlie wasn't surprised, and certainly wasn't keen to be any further involved. Talking it over with the boys the next morning brought a similar response. They had been keen to do something to help, but none of us were going to push in where we were unwelcome.

We would adopt a wait-and-see attitude and carry on at home.

Three days later it rained. Real spring rain, warm and heavy. After doing vital outside jobs like moving the cows, we were all making ourselves busy in the workshop. We do some of our own ATV maintenance, so Jack and Murray were working on four-wheelers and had them in various stages of disarray. Murray had one on its side to grease it, and Jack was deep into the bowels of another, adjusting a something-or-other.

Campbell was fixing drenching guns at the bench under the big window, and I was on the floor welding an underhand cradle for wood chopping.

Above the noise of the welder I was vaguely aware of a vehicle pulling up outside and a door slamming. I carried on, engrossed in what I was doing, and was startled to say the least when I felt a tap on my shoulder. I stopped welding, straightened up slowly as you do with bones like mine, took my welding helmet off and turned around. The bloke standing there was someone I'd never seen before. He wasn't tall, maybe five feet four, but he had a look about him I recognised. Belligerence and aggression coming out of every pore. An Appleby cut from the same mould as the old man.

"Gidday," I said.

"I've come to borrow a couple of dogs," he replied. Now he had an audience, the boys all found things to do within sight of me, and even Georgina, dressed in wet-weather gear on her way back from feeding her chooks, came by.

"And who might you be, coming to borrow a couple of dogs?" I asked.

"I'm Trevor Appleby. I talked to you on the phone a few days ago."

"Yes, you did, and as I recall, seemed to think I should mind my own business." Warming to the cause, I continued. "So I've gone from having to mind my own business to having to lend you a couple of dogs. What's up?"

"There is only one dog at home," he replied, "and he's useless. Won't chase anything, and I want to muster the place. Bring all the sheep in, see what I can sell. I've heard you have twenty dogs, and wouldn't miss one or two for a couple of days."

Georgina and the boys watched our visitor with quiet amusement. Sure, we have twenty dogs. I've three, including semi-retired Liz. Georgina has a young heading dog she's training. Campbell has the most but three of them are pig dogs, useless on sheep. Jack and Murray have a couple each. Useful dogs, but *their* dogs.

"I'm sorry," I said, though I wasn't. "Sure there are twenty dogs here, but they are four separate teams, with twenty separate sets of controls, calls and whistles. Most dogs here won't work for me, let alone some stranger."

Trevor had the decency to look at his feet. He was out of his depth and knew it. He mumbled something about tight-fisted miserable baskets and turned and left us, roaring out of the yard with mud flying from all four wheels.

Georgina was first to recover. "Cup of tea at home in ten minutes," she said, and left to organise it.

"God, give me strength!" Jack spluttered as he ran his fingers through his hair. "That numb-nuts has some people skills." Campbell and Murray made similarly flattering comments and we dashed through the rain to the verandah. Or they dashed and I followed along behind under an umbrella.

"Charlie's just rung," Georgina said as I came in from washing up. "He had a similar visit, only has two dogs, wouldn't lend them, and drew a similar response."

We chatted over the latest developments and when we went back to work were pensive more than angry.

Charlie rang again that night with more news. We get on well with the Durham family but this was a year's worth of phone calls in a week.

"Young Appleby's been trying to muster the farm with a chainsaw."

"What?"

"Yeah, I know," said Charlie. "He was charging about with an old chainsaw, without the bar and chain, yahooing and making a hell of a racket, trying to chase the sheep home."

I thanked Charlie for keeping us in touch and told Georgina what Trevor was up to. The boys, when I told them in the morning, fell about laughing. We wouldn't be the world's best dog handlers or shepherds, but between us we had some fairly able dogs. To go mustering with a chainsaw for noise was certainly a new one on us.

Murray, always on the dry side, said, "I suppose to draft the sheep he would just leave the saw idling at the back of the yards."

We doubted Appleby's tactic would work. When we go scrubcutting with chainsaws and scrub bars the sheep pretty well ignore us after a few minutes. We heard later on the grapevine that's what happened. Another not-so-charitable thought was that young Appleby was in effect going to steal some sheep from his family while no one was there. But of course we don't have uncharitable thoughts.

All these goings-on were intriguing for all of us and the

main source of conversation for hours after each new event unfolded.

We didn't have long to wait for the next. A much more polite Trevor Appleby appeared again a couple of days later. He spoke to the boys down the drive somewhere and Campbell came to see me at the house.

"Trevor's asked for a hand," he said straight up. "I think I'll go over after work and see what he's up to."

"Fair enough," I replied, "can't do any harm. Watch yourself though; he could turn out to be a slippery customer."

XIX

All three boys went over towards the end of the day. I was expecting them to be gone until dark, but they were back in little over an hour.

"We can't muster there," Campbell said, leaning on the back door. "Since we were there last the ewes have started lambing. There's no chance to sort them out until docking at least a month away."

Once the ewes start lambing you can only disturb them gently, you certainly couldn't muster them home, or many lambs would become mis-mothered, separated from their mothers, and generally wouldn't survive as they're too young to wean. Whatever young Appleby wanted to do with them would have to wait.

From what the boys had learnt in their brief look at the Appleby farm with Trevor, he wouldn't be around long. He thought his parents had shot through, so had wanted to take advantage and pinch a few woolly pigs before anybody noticed. But he overestimated his ability to muster. He'd been chased away from the farm by his father as a youngster, and hadn't been farming since. Trevor had told the boys a fair bit in a short time.

Something would have to be done eventually in a month or so when the lambs were old enough to muster and dock. It's not usually that hard. An improved farm has subdivision fences for rotational grazing, pasture and weed control. Paddock fences are designed to run and control yards or races so you can manage stock quickly and easily.

The Appleby place was largely in one paddock. The rough yards at the woolshed were the only yards, and needed work even to function. Rather than an hour or two's work to muster and dock, a good couple of shepherds could take as long as a week or two there and still not get them all.

*

Not a lot happened for a few days, which was how I liked it. The days grew a little longer, the weather became more spring-like. The ewes appeared to be lambing well and it looked like this year's performance would be one of our better ones.

The cows, still being break-fed as they calved, were slow to start, but were now under way and going as well as our cows ever seem too.

Then Malcolm the police sergeant rang and said there were a few small new developments. Could he come and meet with me and Charlie Durham? I said he was welcome to meet here, and a date was made for lunch in a couple of days, and I'd ask Charlie down.

The day and the men arrived and the lunch conversation ranged from local news to the state of rural towns, to the recent woes of the All Blacks and the weather. Which can never please everybody. Then we sat around a table on the verandah so Charlie could smoke. The afternoon was warm and threatened to get moist, but was most pleasant sitting above the river, surrounded by garden and bush.

Malcolm slowly brought the conversation around to the business at hand. "We've been discussing the Appleby disappearance with a wide range of people and it's more difficult than first appearances would suggest." We listened, fascinated I suppose.

"Now obviously either the Applebys have fled for some unknown reason, and this doesn't seem likely as no new reasons have appeared, or more likely they have been the victims of foul play."

Charlie interrupted. "Could they have committed hara kiri?"

"Yes, they could have," answered Malcolm, "but apparently they don't fit the profile of people who do so. We realise that's always a possibility, but according to our sources, it's unlikely to be the case here."

"Which leaves foul play, and we have absolutely no indication of what, if anything, has happened to them.

"Now, our legal people have been doing some research and while the Applebys have been represented by many lawyers in their turbulent past, we have yet to find anyone admitting to being their present legal advisors. We can find no paper trail or wills for instance, in fact anything that can shed any light on either what's happened to them, or what will happen to their estate.

"We've talked to the stock and station industry in the wider area. They have an overdue current account with one large company, which will need sorting out one day, but apart from a number of small bills to pay there appears to be no crushing debt about to swamp the place. There's no receiver waiting in the wings to take the place under control.

"What we have decided to do is attempt to locate the family members, the children, all in their twenties or thirties now we understand, and get them together to appoint someone to manage the place. Not that it will support a manager, but someone has to keep an eye on things, and keep the vital stock work ticking over.

"In the meantime while we try to locate them, and then contact them, it's come to our attention that there's work to be done. It's a farm, for heaven's sake, and farming carries on. To this end we have had discussions with the local AgriQuality manager, and he agrees. One of their staff will spend a few hours soon talking to you local farmers to decide how best to maintain the stock work.

"There may be," he continued, "a need to get some authority to open all their mail. We have done stuff like bank statements to see if their accounts are being used and they aren't. We have looked around for anyone else that may have them under pressure, and can't find anyone."

Charlie was still annoyed about the trees. "What's happened to all the money the Apples would have made from logging all that rimu?" he asked. "That stuff can be worth two or three thousand dollars a cube, and they haven't spent money on the farm. Not that I could see."

"You're right," Malcolm answered. "It's quite possible they have bank account in another town, or could be sitting on a stash of cash that we know nothing about. Similarly with the cash-in-hand proceeds of their little dak-growing enterprise. Where's the money gone?"

"Their house has a lot of expensive toys in it, they are reputed to have traveled regularly overseas, but there are no indications of development or money spent locally.

"We have to accept that as so many weeks, months now, have passed, it gets trickier get to the bottom of this. So we are just going to wait and see what happens in the meantime. But we are going all-out to locate the family, and you may be able help there. We evidently didn't try hard enough earlier, because it's not exactly a close family, as you know, and there's been not a lot of leads to follow up.

"And as I've said, we are getting an AgriQuality livestock guy down here to see you about running the farm, until we can find the family."

I knew they'd have trouble tracking at least one of the family down because he'd changed his surname. The police would have looked at Telecom records to see who had been ringing the Applebys, but no doubt Brent had rung them using a phonecard at a call box. And if the cops had checked to see if any Appleby happened to have flown into the country lately, Brent's change of name could have thrown them off the scent.

I related to Malcolm the visit of Trevor Appleby and said I'd ask the boys right away if they knew where he was from. I went inside to use the phone.

Georgina was telling Malcolm that she was sure there were three children, two sons and a daughter, and that the older son and the daughter hadn't been seen for many years.

I got through to Campbell, who thought Trevor came from somewhere just out of Hamilton, which I relayed to Malcolm.

"He shouldn't be hard to trace," Malcolm said. "Sounds like a delightful character."

Georgina was quite concerned and thinking hard. "You must realise, Malcolm, that in the early years of the Applebys being here we tried hard to make them welcome. But all our hospitality was rebuffed, often rudely. As for the children, we only heard of them, they haven't been here, they never featured. Our family, between us, would know everyone in the valley. Yet the Applebys only came out to functions at which the whole community was involved. We used to feel bad about having failed to get along with them. We really tried, though."

Malcolm told Georgina not to feel bad about it. Between us and the Durham family we had shown more neighbourliness and compassion than anyone he'd heard and seen, he said.

He left to carry on his unenviable task, while we sat talking for a while about whether there was anything else to be done. Nothing was obvious. Charlie left too, and I walked over to the sheep yards where the boys were making quick work of vaccinating hoggets before they settled them in their lambing paddocks, as they'd done with the ewes a month before.

Around half of our hoggets go to the ram, and the dry ones are run off the farm on a pig-infested lease block. I gave them the gist of our lunchtime conversation with the police and Charlie Durham, then left them to take a mob out up the race with old Liz, Ned and Beck, my remaining huntaways.

XX

I came home around six to hear that Bruce, our AgriQuality TB testing man, had already rung, and was ringing back at seven to catch me. He was obviously determined to get on with sorting out the problem of TB testing the Appleby cattle, as he liked to be sure every animal in our valley was done. The other stock work that would be needed was a little out of his league, but he was more than happy to co-ordinate volunteers and help where he could.

In a country where many civil servants were slow at the best of times, it's refreshing to meet one keen and enthusiastic.

Farming our place continued at a quickening pace as docking approached. I made it my job to go over the gear needed to make sure ear markers were sharp, that all the gates for our temporary yards were present and correct — they have a tendency to wander during the year — and that all the supplies we needed were ordered.

When I had 3300 ewes, Georgina, I and two others once did the docking in four and a half days. Now with approaching twice that number it tended to be a long process. The trick to doing it more quickly on our place was pre-mustering the sheep in the larger paddocks into much smaller ones a day or two before we needed to dock them.

It was the boys' call now when to start — when the youngest lambs were not too young, and the oldest not too old. We have four sets of permanent sheep yards as well as the portable ones, and we try to work out of one set at a time so we don't have to shift all the gear too often.

Bruce from AgriQuality came down a day before we started and went with Jack to run the Appleby cattle in to test. After nailing up fallen rails and propping up superfluous gates in gaps so they had holding paddocks, they found and rounded up 35 cattle in half a day and decided that was most likely all. We certainly hadn't seen many during the search. They were mainly older cows with a few younger heifers, and though I didn't see them in the yards it sounded from Jack's description that they could all use a little TLC. Charlie, being a kind-hearted bugger, offered to treat them for lice when they ran the cattle through to read the test. Partly to keep them healthy and partly to keep his own cattle from being reinfested.

Jack ran the cattle in again four days later for Bruce to read the test, and told us that from the look of things the Applebys' lambing was going to be a drawn-out affair. While the oldest lambs were ready to dock, many ewes hadn't lambed yet.

Docking started at our place. For us it's a real family affair. The boys head out early mustering; Georgina, Julia and I follow with a trailer full of gear and smoko. The all-important food and drink. It's hectic bringing the ewes and lambs into the yards, then mundane as we work through them. Huntaways barking, heading dogs dashing everywhere, a cacophony of bleating from the ewes and lambs. The anticipation as we count the tails at the end of each mob to see how many lambs we had docked from the number of ewes counted through the drafting race. Then off to a creek, dam or tap to wash the hands before a cup of tea, a sandwich or three and another mob to bring in.

This year we had an almost clear run of weather and knocked off the ewes in two weeks. Excellent progress, and only the hoggets to go in a couple of weeks more.

Which was lucky because no sooner had we finished than Bruce rang again and wondered politely whether we could lend a hand to do the Applebys'. Yes we could. It had been in our minds for some time and we were prepared for the request.

Knowing what their yards were like, I'd already decided to take over our portable yards so our work over there would be just mustering and docking. Bruce organised Charlie Durham and Fred Clarke and their wives to help, and on a fine Monday morning we attacked.

It was some weeks since our previous tour of the Appleby farm and nothing had changed for the better, but we weren't here to look at that. We had six men with dogs and went quietly so that we wouldn't make all the sheep run away. We started at the most extreme corners of the farm in the morning and mustered back towards the yards. With our hand-held radios, our good keen young men, and a fine clear morning we soon had the whole place done. Well, it's never done really. In this class of country you do your best. And just when you think you've done a hundred percent clean muster, something — some ewes and lambs — will appear from some scrub on a ridge behind you.

We drafted as we docked and took off a couple of hundred dry female and a few male hoggets, put all the ewes dry and wet back with the docked lambs and had the whole job done in about ten hours. Bloody marvellous. Bruce was rapt, I was pleased and even old Charlie had a silly grin on his face. As they say, we repaired to our kitchen and had a few.

Fred brought a dozen cans, Charlie a bottle of the finest, Georgina and I put on more and filled up the gaps with wine and snacks. Bruce, being a responsible sort of bloke, rang his wife and got the okay to stay the night. It was another of those impromptu shindigs that you couldn't pre-plan if you tried . Rightly or wrongly we had done our best for the absent Apples, the more so because Trevor had hardly been encouraging.

XXI

After that we just carried on watching the grass grow and the lambs get fat. Though I'd have to admit, which of course I couldn't, I was increasingly, mildly, troubled by the whole course of events. While I didn't really regret turning a blind eye to what Brent and Jan had done, I was often reminding myself of the old saying, 'Oh, what a tangled web we weave, when first we practise to deceive.'

Malcolm rang. He'd heard of the successful docking at the Applebys' and was generous with his praise. And he'd managed to contact two of the Appleby children and yes, they had arranged a date to come and meet in Taumarunui, to sort out what was to be done. Before Christmas, which was now only a couple of months away.

For some weeks we lost interest in anything off the farm as we struggled with the wet spring weather. To finish calving, to dag ewes, sell fat heifers run through until now to catch the pre-Christmas market. And to catch the before-summer store lamb market. We were busy.

And then only a week before Christmas the Applebys arrived, this time in the form of the ever-surly Trevor, but now with his sister Melanie, who even at a glance was something else. Quite different from all the Apples met thus far. Still in her twenties, smartly presented and easy on the eye, she was obviously in charge of herself and knew where she was going. She was urbane and friendly, chatty even, and Georgina took to her straight away.

Trevor didn't grace us with his presence until later, but Melanie came down to our place to see us as soon as she arrived, to thank us for what we had done. Georgina made light of our efforts, and when I came home they were well into a bottle of riesling and getting along swimmingly.

It soon turned out that beneath her bubbly exterior Melanie too had paid a high price coming into the world as an Appleby, but unlike her brother Trevor she had risen above her unfortunate early years and made a real life for herself. She had her own computer-something business in Melbourne. At twenty-eight. She hadn't been tempted yet by marriage or long-term partnership, a throwback from her upbringing perhaps, and was happy and successful. All these things Georgina had learned in a two-hour conversation. It would have taken me a week.

She had also, I was pleased to hear, been talking to her brother Brent. And try as he might he couldn't be here. Or didn't want to, I thought to myself, quite relieved.

Welcome news continued. Melanie had obviously been in regular contact with Brent and had his written authority to make decisions on his behalf. A mutual respect must exist there. A first for that family.

The even better news was simply that young Trevor was the odd man out. Of the three siblings Trevor was the only one to have not dragged himself out of the mire, was the only one still to hold a grudge against life.

Melanie's sanguine attitude reinforced my quick decision to let Brent and his wife go on home. She had a few bob too, as she was staying in a pub in town, while she and her brother talked with the local authorities about where to lurch to next.

Naturally she made it plain that she was disheartened by the state of her parents' home and farm, and the thought that they had met some untimely end. But only on the surface.

Deep down you could sense a woman very much in control of her life, her feelings and her destiny. The parents who had forced them all out by their deviance years ago would never be forgiven or forgotten. But they would never be missed or angsted over either, at least not by this one.

So Malcolm organised another meeting. This time with Colin Smith the detective, himself, Bruce from AgQual, Charlie Durham, Fred Clark, Georgina and myself. Also invited were the manager of a local stock firm holding some debt, a reliable local agent our family recommended, and a local solicitor in case he could clarify any legal aspects of the situation. And of course the younger generation of Applebys.

We drove to town for this meeting, and it was held on neutral ground in a local hotel's conference room with tea and coffee facilities laid on.

Malcolm, being most involved, chaired the meeting informally. Colin was there to listen, as were we. He started, as you do, by introducing everyone to everyone, then ran through the sequence of events that had brought us together. He was most gracious describing our combined local input and had Charlie, Fred and me all looking at the floor.

He described how the police search had continued quietly looking, checking and prodding, and he was more than frank about their complete absence of success. I suppose we could all privately imagine that they weren't actually trying that hard, but with this family's history, they stayed as thoughts. Quietly and professionally he detailed the whole case, leaving no option unexamined, no cupboard unopened.

You could have heard a snail slithering when the dak operation was described. Malcolm was a total diplomat describing the farm situation, and as neutral as a cricket umpire discussing relationships the Applebys hadn't had.

Then he asked the lawyer to comment. He talked of the lack of precedent. No one had walked off and abandoned a farm in New Zealand for 65 years, apparently. He talked of probate not being granted for five years minimum if no one had been declared dead, and he talked of four of us forming an informal group of trustees to oversee the place until there was some resolution, possibly many years into the future.

Bruce, after doing so much, had little to say. As long as the stock were looked after reasonably well his responsibilities were met. And he hadn't time to do more than he was doing already.

Next was the stock company manager, who seemed embarrassed by the fact he had actually let the Apples borrow any money at all. Their total ignorance of monetary responsibility had been missed by this man when it came to giving credit. To give him his due, he wasn't forcing the issue of repayment quickly in the circumstances. But he was obviously keen to see some resolution as well.

Now it's often been said, that the real decisions committees make are made before or after, but rarely during the meeting itself.

When it came time for our friendly stock agent to contribute, many discussions had gone on before. Between Georgina and me to start with, between me and Charlie and Fred to see if we were on the right track, and between me and our agent of choice, Dave Southern.

Dave was a formidable man to look at, a real front row prop sort of head, with a body to match. The actual guy, like many front row men, belied his looks, with a deep intelligence and in Dave's case, a successful business ethic.

"What I'd suggest is this," he started, "and it's only a few thoughts. Sell everything that's on the farm now. The ewes and lambs will make reasonable money if sold before it gets dry in February. The hoggets will never make you rich, but they will be better sold now, to avoid the work of shearing, dipping, and so on. Mustering, enough said.

"Similarly the cattle. There are not enough to make any real money, and too many to ignore, so sell them too.

"What to do with the grass is easy. Rather than let anybody local get involved with grazing the place, for reasons best not mentioned, I'd suggest getting in some grazing cows from a company I know in Masterton. They'll provide cows, do the work, take all the calves, and pay a set headage for grazing each month, in advance.

"That kills all the birds with three stones," he said, muddling his metaphor. "The stock company can be paid out, local body rates can be paid on time. Any other power charges or outstanding debts can be settled. Remaining cash — and there will be quite a bit — the government, Inland Revenue will want 30%, so keep that much back and do with the rest what you will."

XXII

Dave had left many questions unanswered, and Melanie picked up on a few. “Sound ideas,” she said. “Logistically, though, the farm would need a decent set of cattle yards. Trevor has told me how run-down the place is. On the negative side. On the positive, we wouldn’t have to rebuild the sheep yards or woolshed, which are major jobs.

“My job is in computer technology,” she continued. “I can set up online banking and look after the farm’s accounts. It’ll only take a couple of minutes a week.”

Trevor hadn’t said a word and was well out of his depth, and Melanie seemed to sense this.

She continued again. “If we, you, set up some informal trustees, one with email, I can send you a list of monthly accounts. You can approve them by return email, and I can sort them from my office. Sweet as.”

I was impressed. As much as I was determined my life should be computer-free, cellphone-free and bureaucracy-free, I admired good sense when I heard it. The others were obviously pleased as well.

Except maybe Trevor. He looked lost and broke, and Georgina and I had wondered privately about this.

Melanie again. “Let’s me and Dave do a quick budget. If it turns out there is money from the sale of capital stock surplus to requirements, I could put it to the ‘committee of trustees’, that this money be paid out to beneficiaries, Trevor, Brent and me in equal shares.”

The lawyer wasn't sure about this, and there was a lurking presence here as well. One thought was that the Applebys could somehow return, and the second was that some other debt could surface. At least half of these were legitimate concerns.

Dave Southern pointed out that the income from the cows would be considerable, and then Malcolm got us back on track by calling for nominations for trustees.

I was nominated by Melanie, but declined. I suggested Charlie Durham, Malcolm suggested Dave Southern, because he's a stock agent with his finger on the pulse and with a wide circle of contacts. The main reason it's worth paying a stock agent commission is for his contacts. Georgina was put forward by Fred Clarke, and Melanie herself was an obvious choice. And so it was decided. The future of the Appleby farm in the short term would be worked through by the trustees, with Georgina being chairperson, co-ordinator in charge. She is computer-literate, I hasten to add.

While we all talked over the issues, Dave and Melanie sat away from us at the other end of a long table and drafted up a rough budget.

They quickly came back with a short column of figures. "This is conservative," said Dave, "until I've mouthed a few ewes to check their teeth wear, but we should get:

$60 a ewe for 800 approx	48,000
$50 a lamb for 600 approx	30,000
30 cows @ $450	13,500
5 heifers @ $300	1500
200 mixed hoggets @ $40	8000

"There would be no nett money for wool, as the cost of shearing would more than likely be as much as the wool sale proceeds, but all the sales would yield near enough to $100,000.

"Take off miscellaneous debts, yet to be totalled, of say

$5000, the stock company's debt of $35,000, and there would be a surplus of around $60,000, or $20,000 to each young Appleby. When the probate allows it to be paid out, of course.

"There's no way the money can be paid out until a court rules that your parents are dead. We've heard that there's no precedent for the situation of people walking off the land, not since the Depression anyway. But there's no doubt that selling stock which have no one to look after them is the right thing to do. The main asset is of course the land, which will remain in trust.

"To be prudent, leave say $10,000 in the bank for unknowns like yards, until the cattle money starts rolling, and say $50,000 to disburse. Say $16,000 each. This is a rough budget, with no particular tax complications. The sale of stock could actually achieve more."

Trevor was leaning well forward across the table and having trouble controlling his glee. My guess is that he would have been happy with an potential windfall of $1600, let alone $16,000. He sighed with contentment. "When will this all happen?"

Melanie looked around at us all and Georgina, the new chairperson, took the lead.

"Do we all think that this resolution, to follow Dave's plan, is a good idea?" We all did. The lawyer wasn't used to this degree of pragmatism, but even he couldn't find much fault.

"Over to you, Dave," said Georgina.

"Well, I can actually sell most of them on the phone tonight," he said. "There's strong demand for ewes and lambs at the moment, strong inquiry." Good stock agents usually know what's wanted when and where.

"Do you want to organise them to be shorn?" Charlie and I looked at each other and shook our heads. "Shearers are flat out at the moment," said Charlie.

"Done," said Dave. "Sold with the wool on. Are the cattle within their sixty days of testing, Bruce?" he asked, seeing money to be made here. Stock agents sell on commission, so they sell quickly if they can. He was on the ball. Cattle being sold from a declared movement control area are required to have a TB test no more than sixty days before the date of sale.

"I think so, but I'll have to check dates on the office computer," Bruce answered.

"Is there any other business we should discuss?" Malcolm brought us all back to order.

No one could think of any at the moment so Georgina, Charlie and Fred toddled off together to the supermarket, while the rest of us moved next door to the bar to continue the meeting more informally.

Colin talked to me quietly as we waited to be served. "There's actually not a lot more we can do. Other than wait for them to turn up, alive or dead. The latter, most likely."

Melanie joined us when we had our drinks in hand and was quite pleased for Trevor, who was on the phone somewhere.

"He's had a hard life, my little brother," she started. "What with leaving home early, getting into all sorts of trouble. He's had a dozen jobs, you know, lost them all. Now he's driving a truck for the Waipa Council and this could be his big break."

"Bloody marvellous," I said. "We don't know anything of your lives before you came here, but it can't have been easy."

"No, it wasn't," replied Melanie, looking at Colin Smith. "It was very hard from as early as I can remember."

"Did you have any specific troubles?" asked the policeman gently.

"Hell, yes," replied Melanie. "But there was a decision I made when I left that I've stuck to. I could have dwelt on our family troubles, but right from when I left home at fourteen I knew that I had to look forward. I knew from school that all parents weren't as evil as ours. So I've really put it all behind me. I'll never forgive them, I never could, but equally, I wasn't going to let it ruin the rest of my life. Look at Trevor. He's had real trouble coping. Getting money from the olds will mean little to Brent and me, but it could nearly change Trevor's life. It also means him getting one over the old man. Which never would have happened if he'd been alive."

We both looked up at that remark, Colin especially, because until now, even though most of us thought the Applebys were dead, no one had said it outright.

Melanie recovered quickly and tempered her comment. "What will happen to the decisions we have made this afternoon if, somehow, they return?"

Colin suggested worrying about that when and if it happened, and I wondered how much the police really knew of the Applebys' past, and if like a lot of us they weren't exactly mourning their passing, or for that matter looking too hard for them.

Colin thanked us all and wished Melanie and Trevor well, then left to drive back to Wanganui. Melanie was staying on the premises and had invited Trevor to do the same, offering to shout him, so we organised another round and waited for the shoppers to come back.

Trevor was positively glowing. While showing no repentance for his earlier behaviour, he was a different person. Some money to look forward to, friendly faces around him, and some resolution to problems that had haunted his entire life. He didn't think his parents were alive either.

For the first time in a long time I started having real doubts about what I'd done. Was there in fact a more cunning plot here that I'd fallen into, through my own naivety, my over-readiness to cut people a bit of slack? There was now a whole new attitude of optimism surrounding these kids and that at least was refreshing. Had the three of them been in it together, or had Brent got them on-side after the event as he had with me?

I decided not to push the conversation in any particular way. In fact I couldn't. There were too many people now enjoying themselves.

Dave Southern and Bruce rejoined us and had good news. Some of the sheep were sold already, and the cattle were within the 60-day testing period and could be sold. When could we muster them? I said I'd let them know after I'd talked with Charlie, Fred and the boys at home.

Melanie and Trevor were talking earnestly together, slightly separate from us now, and again I couldn't get over both the difference between them and the change that had come over Trevor. He'd better not drink too much, as the excitement of what had happened was getting to him. Malcolm joined them and I hoped that his mature policeman type attitude would slow Trevor down.

Then Melanie joined Dave and me and the conversation turned to her business in Melbourne. Luddite that I am, it was obvious she was doing well. She mentioned staff doing a dependable job in her absence, she mentioned modern things like broadband and virtual offices that I had little idea about so kept quiet, and she just exuded confidence.

Georgina and the others arrived back and after one drink she proposed we all stay in town for dinner. Good plan. She and Melanie got on famously, as usual. I sat between Dave and Malcolm, with Trevor, then Georgina, Melanie, Charlie and Fred. And a convivial meal it was too. I had plenty of farm business to talk over with Dave and interesting things to discuss with Malcolm. We were certainly in with a group of people who would normally never associate together, but as we all had a common interest it went well.

I'd stopped drinking before dinner so I could drive home, Dave too as he had the usual stock agent's phone work to do half the night, but the others were enjoying some quality wine. Trevor had slowed down, possibly the police influence, but also because he was a changed man. He was happy. In a short week or two he'd gone from being a stroppy grunter to being happy. You had to see the transformation to appreciate it.

We got up to leave for home at a reasonable hour and the day's biggest surprise was about to come. As we stood on the hotel steps saying our farewells, being thanked one by one by a grateful Melanie and an ebullient Trevor, Melanie came up to me, last in line to go down the steps. She raised herself up to kiss my cheek and whispered quietly. "Thank you so much for everything, Tony, and especially thanks for being so understanding with Brent and Jan."

Then she was gone.

XXIII

I stood gaping for five or possibly fifteen seconds, then joined the others in the car. She had known all along.

On the way home Georgina filled in many of the gaps. It's an hour's drive at night, and we always chatted as we drove. She had obviously had a quiet heart-to-heart with Melanie at their end of the dinner table and found out more about the Appleby children's years of abuse. She would not discuss specifics with Charlie and Fred in the car, but left us in little doubt that it was a wonder the children had survived at all.

Fred and then Charlie started snoring quietly in the back. I spent the last half hour of our journey home singing to Georgina a few Irish songs my mate Peter Brook had taught me. Peter, who lives at the head of the valley and is a descendant of the original owners of our farm, is an asset to the valley and especially round the brazier of an evening with a group of friends. Right now his songs were just what I needed to take my mind off certain other matters.

*

We wound down to Christmas in a hell of a rush. In other words, our farm's frantic pace finally slowed and stopped, and we were pleased to be joined by our friends and relatives from Rotorua, Ernie and Adeline, for what is thankfully a relaxing time of the year.

Addy is Georgina's sister and she and her husband Ernie have been through thick and thin. Even after months of not seeing each other we take up together as if it was only a few minutes or a day or two, and we ignored each other's human failings and admired each other's strengths.

Ernie and I had been known in our youth to have caused the odd bottle a bit of trouble, and I quietly hoped that our health and stamina would prevail so we could get in a little trouble again.

The women traditionally planned and prepared a culinary spectacle, while the men did the important work like discussing the exchange rate, the progress of our businesses, and making sure none of the grog went off through too much ageing.

On Christmas Day itself, if the weather was salubrious, we liked to dine in the shade of a silk tree, but at least half the time Huey forced us inside to eat around an extended and bounteous table. The meal could be relied upon to be a success and inevitably lasted a few hours. Often ending up dancing around a crowded floor and the odd younger person crash-tackling the Christmas tree. I'm constantly dismayed at these festive times how the bad habits of the mother come out in the children.

Boxing Day's a sedate affair, recovering in the morning and watching cricket on the box in the lazy afternoon. To ensure no one gets any extra sleep there are usually a few clay targets shot, and to ensure the fish get no sleep there are a few golf balls driven into the river. Aimed at the other side, of course.

January rolls along quickly, and with it the weaning of the last lambs, shearing all the lambs not already sold, and dipping anything else to keep the dreaded fly away. And preparing ourselves for February, which for the last three years has been Georgina's and my time away.

I've always worked through the summer, I've always worked all winter and I've always worked the other seasons as well. I used to be proud of being a worker and I'm sure it's brought us economic success. But I remember wiser heads telling me years ago that nothing is as important as your health. When you are young and fit, being old is yonks away. Now I'm nearly there and so many bones are shagged, I'm not proud of having pushed myself so hard any more. Too much bloody pain.

So Georgina and I bought a boat, and sail away in February for weeks at a time. It's a solace to the heart and soul.

Januarys are busy. We don't have to rush around doing 'last minute jobs', as farming just goes on and there's plenty of people about home to ensure everything's well done. I've always liked to do things my way, but I'd be flattering myself if I thought any more that my way was the best way.

We made sure though that I'd seen the entire farm with Campbell, as he is the stock manager, and between us all we talked over the work to be done in February. The weather is vital, as on our farm we make no hay, silage or other crop. The topography doesn't allow it. So we build up a surplus bank of grass ahead of the stock and watch the weather. Last February was a record wet period, huge flooding down country, record rain here. The February before was record dry and some concern to young farmers not used to a prolonged dry period.

Georgina and I set off to Tauranga, looking forward with restrained glee to our coastal cruising and whatever delights that turned up. We are commonly difficult to prise away from our home, farm and garden, but once away we are sure to enjoy ourselves.

We talked to the boys two or three times a week and watched the weather as all canny sailors and farmers do. In fact I habitually listened to the marine forecast for where we were, and to the King Country forecast for home.

On the East Coast we had balmy weather, light winds and a gentle swell, while at home the boys were finding things getting fairly dry. Our farming relies on regular rain and they weren't getting quite enough. Jack had nipped around with the digger in January cleaning dams, drains and water holes, and we had previously fenced off some of the better dams to keep stock out. We pipe water out to troughs from these fenced dams.

Also the feed — grass growth slows as it dries and the stock management pressure increases.

Campbell and Julia were helping the Department of Conservation do a blue duck survey on the Retaruke River which flows into the Whanganui. There was much less water there than usual, so they were having to portage their canoes frequently in the shallow river reaches.

Georgina and I were in the habit of turning our cellphone on from seven to nine p.m. every evening, in case anybody needed to talk to us. It normally rings at the last moment, which is fair enough, the boys are pretty casual and are quite happy being on their own. I knew when Campbell rang on the dot of seven that something was up.

The Applebys had been found. Or more precisely, the remains of two badly decomposed carcasses had been found, and they were presumed to be the Applebys.

XXIV

"Were they found together?" I asked.

"Close together," said Campbell. "Tied together, actually. The cops have to get a helicopter down into the gorge to recover them. Hell of a job, but there's no other way to get there."

"Bloody hell! What else can you tell me?"

Campbell was almost breathless with excitement. "The police I've talked to say it's murder — double homicide."

"Why?" I was flabbergasted.

"The bodies were weighted down by bulldozer sprockets tied to their bodies with barbed wire. Hardly a suicidal plan, you'd think."

"Bloody hell," I said for the second or possibly third time and noticed Georgina staring at me, needless to say unaware of what was going on. I put my finger over the phone and told her briefly that the Applebys' bodies had been found. Campbell was talking again.

"We were canoeing through a deep part of the Retaruke and saw them, just below the water surface. Scary. There's not much left, the eels have been well fed," he said with typical sensitivity.

There wasn't much more to say. He didn't know any more details. We talked of the farm briefly and hung up. I brought Georgina up to date with most of what Campbell had told me. She sat down, quite upset with the fact it was murder. She no longer had any sympathy for Appleby senior, after spending so much time with Melanie, but was horrified at the thought of anybody being murdered. I didn't tell her about the eels.

We discussed whether we should return home immediately and decided against changing our plans. There was little we could do to help anyway. And by the time we got there it might be all over.

My mind was whirling. I'd thought all along that Brent and Jan had done the Applebys in as a result of very unfortunate circumstances, that in a strange but real way was justified. This was not the case at all. I'd been duped, sucked in, fooled, whatever, and I didn't like the feeling. But then I asked myself, what has changed? Murdered is murdered is dead. And however they were killed didn't trouble me overly. Yeah, I know arseholes have just as much right to live as anybody else, legally speaking. But do they? And do they in this case?

We continued cruising up the coast, calling in here and there and spending nights in bush-lined bays in clear water. Spending quiet time together, feeling a huge sense of achievement as we found new places, facing challenging times together when the weather was rough. Crossing the Colville Channel I'd had a learner's introduction as to why you need to relate the weather forecast to the tides. If the tide is going out and the wind is coming from the opposite direction, the waves can become much higher than the swell forecast would have indicated they were going to be. This phenomenon had caught us out a couple of times. Just about tipped the yacht over once, so now we were much more careful, attentive, and didn't rush to appointments if conditions were inclement. We are in truth fine-weather sailors. Amateurs.

Though we were relaxed and enjoying ourselves, there was a sense of nagging worry beneath the surface. When the weather reports started talking of cyclones building around Samoa and the Cook Islands, by virtually unspoken agreement we turned south and set sail for home.

Leisurely of course. There is no rushing coastal cruising with our limited experience of yachting. In a week or ten days we were up Tauranga Harbour, home port. We arranged for a couple of maintenance jobs on the boat to be undertaken by a local boatbuilder and a marine engineer, packed our kit into the car and drove away with mixed emotions.

After a trip to the supermarket to stock the boot with provisions for the larder, and then a six-hour drive, we arrived home on a late summer evening to a busy place.

Shearing two-tooths was just completed and wool had to be carted to town. Life on the farm rocked on. During our first catch-up with the boys I quickly caught up with the state of play and there was little new. The bodies' identities had been confirmed. They were the Applebys and this was no suicide or unfortunate accident. There was no conclusive evidence of exactly where or how, but there was no doubt that it was murder.

The police had been back with a brief flurry of activity after the bodies had been found and recovered. But after going over all the old ground, nothing new had turned up.

The boys had been on the Applebys' farm only once since we had left home, to receive the grazing cows and show the graziers around the farm. The cows had settled in happily and they hadn't brought on too many, which is often the first mistake inexperienced operators make.

I spent a few days on the digger, catching up with roading and track maintenance, cleaning out more dams for stock water and preparing a new fence line. It quickly became obvious that the digger tracks needed a birthday treat and would have to be taken off the machine and delivered to a Hamilton company for a rebuild.

I made the necessary arrangements and with Jack's help stripped the tracks from the machine and loaded them on the truck to drive north.

We got back to our family weekly meetings the night before I was due to have the tracks rebuilt. Quite opportune, as I'd be away three or four days, depending on what mechanical complications arose.

Campbell, our stock manager, had suggested that our meetings remain alcohol-free until the important issues had been discussed. Quite rightly, as grog tended to make meetings drag on. That's not to say we couldn't have a drink after the first half hour, and that's what happened. We quickly got through the next week's work plan, then talked over pending stock and wool sales so Georgina could manage the cash flow. And opened a couple of beers.

I'd noticed Campbell being even more thoughtful than usual during the afternoon, and with a beer in hand he decided to open a new line of thinking.

"What do you guys think of the Applebys' dak-growing scheme?" he asked.

"Not a lot," said Jack. "They could have easily killed themselves."

"You're not wrong there," said Campbell. "But for all their stupidity, Apple was a cunning old rogue."

"What are you thinking?" I asked.

"I'm not sure, and I'm no detective," Campbell answered. "It's just something there doesn't ring true."

Georgina had been listening, and you could feel her senses quickening. "If you think there's more involved, call Colin Smith and tell him," she suggested.

"Maybe," said Campbell, looking towards the window. "But I've got nothing definite, I've never actually been inside the cave, and I'd like to."

We all considered what he seemed to be suggesting and without anybody saying anything, knew it could be a worthwhile idea.

"There's certainly no harm in going to cast a beady eye,"

I said, with more confidence than may have been justified in the circumstances.

"Go together," said Georgina, intuitively.

Jack wandered over to the shed to put a spare ATV battery on the charger to drive their spotlighting light, and we left it at that.

Except I didn't head north in the morning as planned. I decided that the truck shouldn't take such a long trip without a thorough service, oil and filter change. On this flimsy pretext I stayed home and worked around the shed on the truck. Waiting to see if Campbell's worries would amount to anything.

They did. Within two hours of leaving after breakfast, the boys were back and bursting. It's uncanny how you can tell by the way a vehicle is driven that something is up.

XXV

In seconds Campbell, Jack and Murray were beside me.

"There's human bones buried in Apple's cave," Campbell blurted out.

"There are metal anchors screwed into the rock walls," Murray continued, his eyes still popping.

"That mad Flynn went berserk," joined in Jack. "He was tearing at the ground and running round in circles."

"Slow down, slow down, start at the beginning," I said, wiping my hands on an old shirt.

It had been Campbell's premonition or suspicion or whatever, so he took control.

"Something's been niggling me for a while," he began. "Nothing specific, not even a real idea. Just a few things that didn't fit. When we went in the cave I wasn't really thinking marijuana; I wasn't thinking anything. But it's not obvious. It's there. So we walked in with open minds. Murray noticed the bolts screwed into the walls straight away. And there was a funny smell coming from some ground that had been dug up. A hint of rotten meat smell, you know, like an offal hole. Flynn started digging and scratching."

Flynn is Campbell's *numero uno* pig dog and has some unusual habits. Often when fed he would bury his meat to eat later, whereas most dogs chomp through it as quickly as possible.

"Flynn's pulled up some bones that don't look like animal bones to us."

"This is not in our league," I said. "Let's get on the blower." So off to the house. The boys couldn't sit still, knowing something big was up.

I put on the jug and rang Malcolm. I hadn't talked with him for weeks and as soon as he heard my voice he wanted to catch up. I let him go through the phone rituals for a couple of minutes and got down to ruining his day.

"What made you go back to the cave?" he wanted to know.

"Not 'go back', we've never been in there before. Campbell just thought there was something up, and the hunch wouldn't go away." I looked at Campbell pacing the room.

"I'll get back to you," Malcolm said and hung up.

We were no sooner sipping tea than the phone went and it was Colin Smith. I put Campbell on, since it was his idea, and he went through the sequence of events. He listened for a few moments, saying "Sure" and "No trouble" and "Good as wood", as Colin talked to him.

He hung up the phone and said, sort of annoyed but in fact quite pleased with himself, "I've shagged up the rest of the day. Malcolm's already on his way and I think Colin's going to fly up. They'll want transport, a generator. They'll be here in an hour."

They were. Malcolm arrived first with the same police-woman, Sharon Lysaght, but before they had even caught their breath there was an unmistakable *wop-wop* of a large helicopter. Colin stepped out carrying a bag and helped unload more gear. Another bloke passed him equipment and the pilot shut the machine down.

Jack and Murray had spent a little time locking up dogs, fueling bikes and hooking up trailers, and were ready to go. Campbell was explaining the sequence of events. The new guy was introduced, asked where the site was and quickly showed a few signs he knew his business. "Can we not fly my equipment right there?" he asked. We had a quick confab and said yes. To within a couple of hundred yards. So the gear was loaded back on the helicopter. Which wound up and took off again.

I rode along slowly, more occupied by what had gone on and how I'd reacted to that than thinking about where I was going. One or two things were painfully obvious to me, and as the plot got increasingly complicated, was I digging myself into an even deeper hole?

XXVI

It was looking as though, counting the Applebys dead, there were going to be several more bodies, who knew how many in total. This made the whole murky business into far more than your average domestic killing. This was getting to be up there amongst New Zealand's more heinous crimes, and as such there would be few rocks left to hide under.

Maybe it was time for me to dissemble no more, and at least tell my family how much I knew. How much I'd kept from them. The very thought of this, as it occurred to me, made me shudder. Until now we had no secrets. How would they see me now? Breaching their trust. Concealing a crime, concealing information. Wasting everybody's time.

Time would tell. Meanwhile back on earth I arrived at the spot where the helicopter had landed. The pilot was sitting in the shade of some ponga ferns at the edge of the clearing nearby. I joined him and straight away he wanted to know what was going on. He said he'd been asked to stay away from the cave by the police but, like most of the public with a little knowledge of the Appleby story, was dead keen to know more. Seeing no harm in doing so, I filled him in on events up to now — the broad-brush approach, five-minute summation job — up to the present moment.

We could hear the generator ticking away quietly a hundred metres away; with the long lengths of cable they'd brought, the cave would be well lit. Really, the previous searches of the area had been cursory. Torch-lit, I recalled, and looking for the wrong things. They had been looking for a sophisticated dak operation, hadn't found more than a minor one, and hadn't looked further. Or deeper. Understandable, I suppose.

The police would have arrived at the cave an hour before I pulled up and it was at least another hour's waiting until we heard the generator turned off and voices coming closer. Flynn came straight to me, wagging his tail and jumping around, fired up with the heaps of praise he'd been getting, rolling over and over in the grass.

Campbell sat down beside us and we waited as the police arranged themselves. No one was in any rush any more. Colin Smith told us roughly what they thought they had found.

"The cave floor is basically rock," he started. "Someone's dug holes in the rock and buried bodies there. They are shallow graves, but they have been hollowed out a bit since we were here last. Campbell here thinks there's been a pig rooting about in there, which would explain a number of things, like why we smelt nothing last time. Though caves are dank at the best of times. The graves must have had the dug-out rock tamped down and sort of sealed off."

"How many?" I managed to ask.

"Looks like three, from what we can tell easily," he replied. "We will have to bring a team back, experts, pathologists and the like. Photographers. I imagine we will have to chain gang out all the loose material, expose what's there and determine who they are."

Didn't sound like much fun to me. "What do you reckon has been going on here?" I asked.

Colin looked at the other police before replying. As though getting their approval, or searching for their ideas. "We may never know," was his first reply. Then he carried on. "From all we know of old Appleby's reputation as a boy botherer, these may be boys he went too far with. But appreciate I'm guessing. We have been quietly pursuing our inquiries these last few months, and have built up a fairly ugly picture. It would seem as though he's been pushing the boundaries with teenagers and whoever else he could get his hands on for years. Largely got away with it, as young people aren't too keen on discussing this sort of thing. Look, I'm speculating and we aren't supposed to do that. Let's wait and see what's dug up."

Leaving their equipment in place, they flew straight upwards for ages. I guessed that they wanted to reach a cellphone signal so they could contact their superiors. Campbell and I rode home.

Lunch was a rather subdued affair, once the brief outline of what they'd found was discussed again. I turned on National Radio to catch the long range weather forecast at 12.30 p.m. as I was in the habit of doing. Listened and turned it off.

"Rain coming?" Georgie asked.

"Yes," I replied, and gave the police a brief summary of weather in these parts.

"Shouldn't worry us much," Colin answered. "An event of this size, there will be no problem getting support helicopters and whatever we need."

"So you won't be worried by a bit of mud then?" Georgie said.

"Not at all, in fact we will hardly need to bother you. If we can load out whatever we find there, we'll be sweet."

After a while the police left. They would be back tomorrow and felt they didn't need to secure the scene, as only we few knew anything was going on.

I wandered over to the shed, then to the dog kennels … and made a decision. There could be little sense in involving everyone at this stage, or implicating anyone else in my decision to let Brent and Jan Appleby off. I'd talk about it with Georgina tonight and go from there.

We'd been together for too long to do it any other way. What had been discovered wasn't what I'd expected. I mucked around for the rest of the day feeling restless, doing fill-in jobs, mowing the grass, leaving till dinner time the big job ahead.

We've developed bad habits during some of our meal times, reading or watching TV as we eat. There's nothing like spreading the *Herald* out and moving your plate to turn the pages. Tonight was different, we already had enough to talk about and speculate over. And all along I was struggling to know where to begin. So eventually I just did.

"You remember the day I went looking for cows up the Kaiwhakauku Stream?" I started half way through our meal. "There's something I haven't told you about, and I'm sorry. Sort of. My motives for keeping this from you weren't selfish, and nothing to do with trust. Rather a spur of the moment thing."

XXVII

Georgina looked at me in a most unusual way as I continued to describe what had happened all those months ago. It was a look I hadn't seen before, and as I continued there was the odd little barely concealed grin. My story didn't take long, as she knew most of it. Other than my concealment of the early stages.

Without much acknowledgement she stood up and began taking our plates over to the sink. I sat motionless, worrying feverishly as she rinsed and placed them in the dishwasher. Then she came up behind me, her reflection in the windows over the table, and put her hands on my shoulders.

She could barely suppress her laughter, and I had no idea what was coming next.

"I'm so relieved," she finally said. "You've been so preoccupied these past months, I thought much worse was happening."

"I didn't know I've appeared preoccupied."

"Of course you have. We've all noticed something was up. Both boys have mentioned it. Campbell thinks you're worried about his stock management skills. Jack thinks you've had enough of farming. And I must admit I thought you might be having some mid-life crisis. An affair, even."

"Christ," I said looking straight at her in the reflection. "An affair, me? Chance would be a fine thing."

"Yeah, perhaps." Georgina sat beside me. "But you haven't been yourself for months."

"Maybe not," I acknowledged, not realising the truth of

what she'd said. "But what do you think of what I've done?"

"Rash, probably, unwise for sure … and maybe the only thing you could have done," she replied.

"How do you mean? Explain yourself."

She sighed and leaned back, composing her thoughts. "I've met two members of the Appleby family lately," she started, "and they have had a hell of a start to life. There seems little doubt that Mr Bad Apple has put a blight on many a young chap's future, and now we find he's more than likely a murderer or worse. If he were alive he would be before the courts, fighting for his survival for years.

"This way, your way, he's dead, punished, finished with and only his victims have suffered."

"My way maybe," I said, "but when I told them to go I'd no idea, for one, that Brent and Jan had carefully and calculatedly murdered them, and for two, that there were other deaths."

"Fair enough," said Georgie, "and I certainly don't believe in taking the law into your own hands. But in this case maybe it's the best outcome."

I was stunned to silence by the logic. Simply because we'd been together so long our thought processes were similar in many ways, yet so independent in others.

"So before we go any further," I said, "like discussing what's next, what do you really think of what I've done?"

"I'm pleased you've told me, I'm pleased it was nothing else worse. It was your decision in the spur of the moment, so let's see if we can live with it. Exactly as you have done until now."

"A problem shared is a problem halved, usually, although sometimes I've found it's a problem doubled." I mooched over and put the kettle on. A cup of tea is the best thing to follow an evening meal.

"Let's go back to being logical," Georgie started again, and

I sat back down. "The senior Applebys have caused everyone grief. Tradesmen, neighbours, shearers, their 'employees', mostly their family, and that's without them having killed anybody. So how can they be better off by having a murder investigation now?"

I pondered this for a while, got up and put two cups on the table, saw the look and fetched saucers. Made some weak black tea and sat down again.

"What about the rest of the family?" I asked, meaning the boys.

"Don't say anything to anyone," Georgina replied immediately. "You know, I know, that's enough. The rumour mill in the valley is already working overtime."

"Aren't we setting ourselves up as judge and jury?" I asked.

"Maybe," Georgina replied. "But maybe not. You've obviously thought this through since you first got involved. You haven't killed anybody, abused anybody. You don't actually know who killed Mr and Mrs Appleby. Who's to say the three kids weren't involved together? Really, what can be gained by having the young Applebys dragged before the courts? It won't bring anybody back."

"Yeah, I suppose you're right. So it's good riddance to bad rubbish, do ya reckon?"

"In a way," said Georgie, "but let's wait and see what the police discover. They are much too decent to be mucked around — I think you've helped, rather than hindered them. If anything they find changes our point of view, we can always change tack. Otherwise it's our secret."

As I've said, this wasn't the outcome I'd expected. Life sure is full of surprises. But was it right, morally? Or did we care?

*

The police arrived back in force the next day. The same helicopter crew and a total of ten officers. They left three four-wheel drive vehicles at our place and the chopper ferried three or four loads of people and equipment to the cave area. We stayed out of the way, waved as they went past, carried on with our work, knowing there was little more we could do.

The phone was ringing at the main house, with our various neighbours wondering what all the latest fuss was about. Georgie gave a brief explanation that the police had found something interesting to look at and said we'd let them know when we heard anything.

Everybody was chewing on their cud, so to speak. Especially Campbell, who had instigated this latest action, wondered what sort of wasps' nest he'd opened. The rest of the family wondered how much lower the Appleby family could go. Gloom was in the air.

Halfway through the arvo the helicopter wopped into the dog kennel paddock. Sergeant Malcolm jogged over to our house to make a few arrangements. Like how many people could we accommodate in our shearers' quarters. The job they were doing was going to take them longer than expected. We assured them there was heaps of room, that grub would be no problem, and set about putting a few beers in the quarters' fridge.

Georgie organised a hand from Andrea and Julia for an elaborate country meal and soon after five o'clock, beer o'clock, they were back in dribs and drabs, one load at a time. The showers worked overtime for a while, and a congregation began on the deck.

No one had enjoyed their day, but with so many people about it was natural that the evening became something of a social occasion. Ten of them and six of us, and the odd box of beer after a hard day.

The police were being super-cautious, had endured a

nightmare of a time, were quite keen to take their minds off what they had encountered. We, on the other hand, were split between the younger generation bursting to find out what was discovered, and Georgina and me not really wanting to know.

Other than those police people we had already met, the rest were made up of experts drawn from major cities, although two were just there to be navvies. Carrying the diggings outside in sacks. Seems crude, but there was no way machinery could be employed.

The younger people, kept together by age and sociability, soon left the few older ones behind, so four of us old goats ended up sitting in a corner of the quarters' deck with a jug of water and a bottle of better-than-average whisky. It seemed from my listening position that there was one relatively 'fresh' body; the others unearthed so far had been there for years. Photographing, checking and recording body and dental details was the job on hand and I was really pleased not to be involved. It also seemed to be the consensus that the Applebys had done them in by means yet to be determined, and as the Applebys were deceased the full story would likely never be known. No doubt there'd be a pro forma investigation — everybody wants 'closure' these days.

These worthy police people seemed to think that it was an open-and-shut case of serial killing, that had been brought to a close by an unknown agent who had saved them a lot of bother, truth be told.

While they made no pretense of being able to speak on behalf of their superiors or the crown prosecutor, they didn't think a murder investigation would go very far.

Finding the families of those dead here would take ages and would be priority. Apparently many people go missing every year and just disappear, in what are usually innocent circumstances.

There was much discussion about how the Applebys had lured these people to their remote farm, but those who had met the Applebys knew though that they could appear quite credible at first encounter.

Speculation continued quietly during the long and increasingly mellow evening. Talking in bed later, Georgie and I agreed that it was well and truly in the hands of police now. We nodded off to the sound of moreporks calling to each other in the bush across the river.

EPILOGUE

Two of the bodies found in the cave were eventually identified from dental records; the other one remains unknown. The two were young males from Auckland who had long left their homes after difficulties with their parents. One of them had been last seen sleeping under a motorway flyover, and both had police records from having been arrested for 'loitering with intent' and some less savoury misdemeanors. Both had been known to supplement their dole payments by allowing themselves to be picked up by men in ill-lit corners of the city.

The coroner found that the Applebys were murdered by a person or persons unknown. The police file stays open.

After all the usual circus the farm was sold, no doubt to the immense satisfaction of the young Appleby conspirators, and the new owners are gradually bringing the property to rights.

Life in the valley has outwardly returned to normal, but there's not quite the same ingrained level of trust among the valley-dwellers now. Everybody suspects that somebody must know something. Murray's farewell went off like a rocket, no doubt releasing some of the underlying tensions of the preceding months, but the conversations were dominated more by analysis of the murders than by his academic prospects.

As for Georgina and me, our marriage has subtly morphed — at times there is a barely perceptible extra bit of distance between us. Occasionally one of us is caught looking sideways at the other, and the expression I see on her face I can't always decipher. And I see Lizard giving me a funny look now and then. No need for her to get uppity; she was there and she heard every word, so she's just one more accessory after the fact of murder.

… & other stories

Dick Barrett

To develop our first farm at Mamaku we did all sorts of work. We carted hay in the summer; cleared land by felling trees which we cut up, split and sold as firewood in the winter; built a house and farm buildings; fenced paddocks; created pasture and otherwise improved our land in any spare time available. It was back-breaking work, often very wet, frustrating even. But always satisfying and over a long period quite rewarding. The profits were largely, I would have to say, the result of buying undeveloped land, doing it up and selling it. All the sweat really just made the payments to keep us current with the bank.

Over the years at Mamaku we employed many people, some of whom were a tremendous help and good fun. Every now and again, usually in deepest winter, I'd end up by myself, trying to do it all on my own. It was usually too wet to be very productive and I was always behind with the firewood orders.

Solace was often a few beers on the way home at the Mamaku Club while having a yarn with friends and neighbours. This is where a long association with Dick Barrett began.

You can imagine the situation. I was halfway down the second jug after a hard day, talking work with my neighbour Alistair and bemoaning the fact that I was two weeks behind, when Dick, who I had only briefly met, interrupted.

"I'll give you a hand."

The offer barely registered, the conversation ebbed and flowed as Dick sat listening. He listened a lot. During a lull, most likely when Alistair was away refreshing jugs, Dick said again, "I'll give you a hand."

More alert this time, I replied immediately, "Can you drive a truck?"

"Sure, done little else, graders, dozers, trucks. Bored in retirement, couple of days a week would be good."

"How much money, what would you want an hour?"

"Nothing. You need a hand, I'm doing nothing, let's see what happens."

After another jug or two and more talk I went home and next morning at 8 a.m. collected Dick and began a friendship that would last many years.

He was a quiet bloke, diffident among strangers, but an amazingly good driver of any vehicle or machine. Good company too. Often after our weekly session at the club he would really surprise me with an ability I would admire. Or two abilities. He had an amazing capacity to drink beer, age never slowed him, and he had an even more acute ability to sum people up.

I have only ever had old gear. Secondhand trucks and tractors, and at that time a third- or fourth-hand bulldozer. Dick used it to cut tracks you would swear had been graded; he winched logs, winding in the winch rope without damaging so much as a strand of wire, and he never broke anything.

He was never late. Long days, long sessions, he was always reliable.

During quiet times, while we were repairing something, having lunch or maybe driving the truck home in the evening, Dick told me the story of his life.

I have no intention of going into his personal trials and mistakes, but he told stories as he went of interludes that really tickled my fancy. Stories of when his mother-in-law died, or when he killed all the village cats, or how he showed people my dog's tricks, and the one about the lemon tree, kept me amused for hours and I still laugh about them when they cross my mind.

Dick married Dot later in life; he had a previous family somewhere down south. Dot's parents — particularly her mother — were, according to Dick, the in-laws from hell. In a not-unheard-of theme, Dick's mother-in-law had to be the meanest woman in the world. When the old chap died and his estate was settled there was not much left to go around; the old lady was skint. Dot decided therefore that her mother should come to Mamaku and live with them. Dick didn't have much say in the matter.

I should point out here that Dick's what I would call a shed person. At any home they owned his vital accessory was a decent shed where he could collect things, for he was a magpie, where he could stay out of the road and from where he could keep an eye on the world going past his window. Warm in the winter, cool in the summer, home brew bubbling. Dick was only inside the house for meals and sleep.

I would say the mother-in-law had more than a little to do with Dick's wanting to work. He had retired in the normal sense, but was compelled to go back again. She gave him no peace. I suppose many sons-in-law are a trial to their new families. Dick was well into his 60s, no cheeky boy, and partial to a convivial drop or two.

About which she complained, in the time-honoured way. She did not like the way he dressed, the way he treated Dot (always with respect, so far as I could see), how he cut the grass or dug the garden. Anything and everything he did was not up to scratch and Dick was unhappy as a result.

This sorry state of affairs lasted years, not months, so it was little wonder that when Dick awoke one night around 2.20 a.m. and heard the old girl dying he did not rush about.

Rather he paused, listened, and quietly went back to sleep. Now the only person I have actually seen die faded away very quietly, elegantly even. Not so Dick's mother-in-law. She gasped, she groaned, her long sighs became drawn apart; she died in a vociferous manner as she had lived. Not loud enough to wake Dot, but loud enough for Dick to hear.

The next thing Dick remembers was waking up at his customary 7 a.m. to hear Dot in the nearby bedroom imploring, "Wake up mother, I've brought you a cup of tea."

Dick, without thinking, calls out: "Don't worry about giving her a cuppa, she's dead. Died at 2.20 this morning."

There apparently followed a scene of some epic proportions, during which time Dick had some trouble explaining his nonchalance.

Then Dot rang their local doctor, who duly arrived and pronounced the old girl dead, and was somewhat surprised to hear the exact time of death. He was a tad suspicious and called the police. They were equally unimpressed with Dick's story and placed him under house arrest.

The details all checked out and Dick had done nothing illegal. Feathers were slowly unruffled and life returned to normal. Then all the rellies arrived for the funeral, and it turned out the old girl had to be buried in Napier. The undertaker wanted $2000 to cart her there, which caused some consternation amongst the parsimonious.

Again Dick leapt to the rescue. It would give me some pleasure, he said, to carry her to Napier in the back of my ute for $1000. Agreement was quickly reached but the still-lurking police had a different point of view. At that time only Maori could transport their own dead, so Dick's plan to rattle the mother-in-law over every back route to Napier was thwarted.

*

One or two neighbours used to comment that they could set their watches by Dick's passing in the truck on his way to work. He was indeed very punctual. One morning, though, he arrived at work a couple of minutes late and seemed unusually flustered. With a little grin, which meant trouble for someone.

It turned out that he had been asked by Dot to get rid of some cats that kept making a mess in her garden. This was no ordinary garden, however. It was Dot's pride and joy, her life's work, her artistic flair and everything else creative rolled into one. It was a great achievement and stood out proudly in a sombre village as a fine example of how to make a modest house in a modest area a credit to its owners.

But cats were coming to it every night and ruining Dot's hard work and artistry. Why there, who knows, they just had to go. And as Dick was an intrepid ex-possum trapper he was just the one to deal to the problem. He would receive little peace until he did.

Dick went off to his shed, concocted a fabulous lure, laced it with a fair dose of cyanide and laid it where the cats played havoc.

Havoc indeed. On his way out in the morning he glanced behind the spuds to gauge his success and could not believe his eyes.

Thirty-four cats lay dead around the lure.

Keeping his head down, literally behind the hedges around the place so no neighbours could see what he was up to, he crawled around collecting the cats and dragged them to a freshly dug patch of garden where evidence of his deed could be interred.

Buried deep. Fortunately or unfortunately, depending on your love of cats, in his haste to get to work on time after burying the cats, Dick neglected to remove the bait that had worked so well.

That evening he arrived home late, as it was our usual weekly night for a session in the RSA on the way home. Next morning, up early to avoid any trouble by removing the bait, he went outside to find another nineteen cats dead in the garden.

Being the sort of character he is, Dick didn't panic. Another hole, another burial, this time including the bait, then off in the truck.

Dot never knew, no one ever knew; for days there were people roaming around calling "Kitty kitty kitty" and all the things people do. Dick sat tight in his shed, expressed concern, watching the world go by, while in the garden Dot and the flowers flourished.

For a while, between selling one farmlet and building a home on another, our family shared a village life. This offers many advantages over a more remote rural choice, including being able to walk to school, or to the shops, or walk home from the aforementioned club. One distinct disadvantage was the number of roaming dogs and cats. Many feral, but a lot of folk do not realise what their pussies get up to when put out for the night. The sudden decrease in population in Mamaku caused quite a few comments, but no explanation of what happened was ever forthcoming.

*

I had a huntaway dog called Rock. Bought from a retiring shepherd who had trained him expertly, Rock worked really well and had been brought up amongst a family, so as a six or seven-year-old he was invaluable help on the farm and a likeable cove to have around. Dick often took him home on the truck if I was going to be away somewhere, ferrying firewood or hauling hay for instance. When this happened Rock had a little ritual he would perform before retiring for the evening tied up to the back of the truck.

One day after work Dick arrived home, pulled up in his usual place beside his driveway, and parked. Directly in front of the truck were Dot and a neighbour, Mrs Collingwood, leaning on their boundary fence passing the time of day on a pleasant summer's evening.

Dick stepped down from the truck, said gidday, and turned nonchalantly towards Rock on the back.

"Rock," Dick said quietly yet firmly enough to be heard. "Rock, jump down from the truck." Rock did and came to Dick.

"Rock," said Dick. "Go to that lamppost and piss on it." Rock left Dick's legs, strolled to the post and did the duty of all dogs.

"Rock," Dick ordered in a friendly voice. "Leap back on the truck and walk around the deck." Which of course he did. Then the finale. "Rock, lie down and lick your cock." And so it happened. The ladies were shocked, but a fair bit impressed. "Good lord, Dick," said Mrs Collingwood, "what extraordinary control you have over that dog." Dick said something pleasant but non-committal, as was his way, and wandered to the shed for a well-deserved home brew. Rock, meanwhile, carried on doing what he did unbidden every time he went to Dick's place and slept.

*

Dick and Dot eventually moved to Colville, Christ knows why. When we had started looking for a bigger farm, Dick suggested I buy a place with two houses so he could tag along and continue to give us a hand. Kuratau didn't have a spare house, so for some reason the move to Colville was on. We used the flying Bedford to shift their furniture and other gear. Dick did a load one weekend and I followed the next week with another load in the same truck, while Dick and Dot drove their vehicle of the day, a CF Bedford van. I did in the differential on the last hill between Coromandel and Colville and had to be towed the last ten miles or so. As we went through one of those coastal villages there was a crash-tinkle-tinkle behind the truck as some of Dot's priceless bits dropped from underneath the cover and onto the road. A million pieces of broken crockery.

So we arrived in Colville in convoy with my truck under tow. We settled Dick and Dot in, arranged for a local grease monkey to fix my diff, and set off home in Dick's van.

We were busy ourselves moving to a new farm south to Kuratau, and became so far apart we didn't see much of Dick and Dot for a while. There was, however, the odd interesting story we caught up with.

Their new house was just a short distance from the Colville store, which sold everything, as isolated stores do. During the busy summer season cars queued for ages to fill up with petrol and holidaymakers stocked up with supplies.

Dick observed all this from his shed. Typically only in the house at meal times, when he wasn't checking out his new surroundings he was in his shed watching the world go by.

One day the queue from the store stretched well past the Barretts' as people stocked up. Waiting impatiently, folk walked up and down from their cars to the store and back with goods.

One hippie bloke was noticed eyeing up Dick's lemon tree. A huge old tree that took up half the front lawn, with branches laden with fruit, a tree so big you could disappear in it.

Returning from the store with a box under his arm, the hippie type put down the box and climbed the tree. Plastic bag in hand in which to put his booty, a furtive look around to see who was watching, and up he went into the tree.

Quick as a flash, Dick slipped out and pinched the box. An eye for an eye and all that, he thought.

Down comes the hippie. "Where the hell is my box?" First he looks around, mystified, not believing what he is (not) seeing. Dick watches from his stool. The man becomes more agitated, starts going from car to car in the queue. Asking, pleading, complaining. "Where's my effing box?" Up and down he goes, getting more and more steamed. Tempers fray, abuse is thrown, violence threatened… but no box. It sits under Dick's feet with an old grass-seed sack thrown over.

The comedy show goes on for an hour. Dick has a quiet ale, dinner is served, peace settles on Colville.

The next day Dick takes off the grass-seed sack, opens the box, wondering what could be in it that set off such a vitriolic rampage. Several flagons of Old Pale Gold, fortified sherry. Dick invites the neighbour over and it takes the old men two whole days to get through it.

Grass Grubs

We farmed at Kuratau from 1982 and — for people with as little hands-on experience as we had — for some time it was quite a battle.

While in theory the money to purchase the new farm had come from our previous farm at Mamaku, in reality farming there had been very much part-time. Full-time was making money — felling and selling 500 truckloads of firewood each winter, carting hay in the summer, bulldozing, generally keeping the wolf away.

So Kuratau was full on for a while. We started with ten paddocks: watered, but with little shelter for ewes lambing in cold winters, and a history of erratic grazing management. As was the system of the time we rotationally grazed, break-fed stock, made heaps of hay and silage for winter supplement, planted swedes and fenced up new paddocks as fast as we could.

The results were startling and for some time we thought

this farming caper, at least on our place, wasn't so bad. Our per-stock unit performance, per-hectare performance, the real crunch figures, were good. Increasing every year. Life on the farm was challenging, interesting work with a young and growing family.

The first signs of the trouble that I want to tell you about here started in a small way. There was no cause for alarm. I suppose many troubles don't send out warning signs, or especially warning signs that the young and inexperienced could recognise. I'd agree with the at least ten million people who acknowledge that hindsight is a wonderful attribute.

The farm had a two-kilometre southern boundary of bush and scrub. Scrub at one end to bush at the other, in a perfectly straight line running damn near east to west. In the autumn and winter of 1985 we noticed areas of grass dying along the bush/pasture margin. When it shouldn't have been. Not just dying but becoming soft to walk on, obviously easy for marauding wild pigs to rip up. In other words, a mess.

A lack of grass growth was quite serious. The initial area affected was perhaps five hectares. Immediately conscious that there was something amiss underground, we began a seven-year campaign against grass grub. As this doesn't pretend to be a scientific description of anything, I don't intend to concern you with the various varieties of grass grubs, their scientific or Latin names. Whatever they are called they all do similar pasture damage, causing equal economic havoc.

First efforts at control were modest, as we had no inkling of where we were heading, I first fed out hay or silage on the affected areas so that stock would concentrate their weight there and push topsoil back into place, and there would be some reseeding as well. It was too little, too late. By next autumn the damage had spread to at least 50 hectares, and down the lines of the prevailing wind there was noticeable damage as well.

We have always, Rachel and I, been tree planters and these evil beetles — that the grubs grow into — were stripping our little trees. Bare. They were everywhere. On the windward side of trees they flew all over the new growth of the eucalyptus, blowing over the bluffs and fattening the trout of Lake Taupo with a huge harvest. The grass continued to die.

My sister Rosemary called by about now and told me of a Dr Trevor Jackson she had met on some course at Lincoln University, who was experimenting with some form of biological control. Few details available.

Pigs came out at night and ripped up whole paddocks, and bulls we had decided to farm for profitability ripped holes everywhere in the easy digging. The problem was getting serious.

We were in a regime of fattening everything, growing bulls at a great rate, ploughing rough paddocks to put in crops of swedes, which when eaten off were put into new pasture.

So we investigated types of grass that grass grubs wouldn't eat. At a premium price per kilo we bought and sewed resistant varieties of ryegrass, cocksfoot and Yorkshire fog, Phalaris and chicory. To some extent these measures helped, except that cultivation itself didn't improve things.

Some more technical stuff here, briefly. In the days when Lands and Survey Department farmed this land, grass grubs were also a problem. In those days from around the 1960s onward it was good farming practice to apply DDT pellets to the pasture. This DDT wiped out the grass grubs, no worries. Grass grubs are a New Zealand native that are kept in control naturally by a number, at least two, pathogens that make them crook and limit procreation. DDT took out the grubs sure enough, but it also took out the pathogens. After many years the grass grubs came back, but the pathogens were still dead.

More seriously, the DDT was detected in milk and meat

exported overseas, so use of the chemical was banned. Alas, the imbalance the use of DDT had caused in our soil infrastructure had a long way to go before it was corrected.

About this time we started noticing large areas of our swede crops dying as well. At first we blamed turkeys: a good neighbour, Dick Truebridge, had in 1982 released a few turkeys for the hell of it; maybe he liked the taste. They revelled in the Kuratau climate and were soon numbering 300, in three flocks.

Seeing the dead swedes and noticing turkeys amongst the swedes was enough to decide they had to go. And go they went. Shotguns, rifles, trucks. For a while the only good turkey was a dead one. Unfortunately for them, the swedes kept dying. More level heads prevailed when a closer inspection found up to 25 grass grubs eating the bottoms of each and every swede in the dying patches. Having no grass to chew, the little bastards had quickly changed their diet.

One of the most successful pathogens, Serratia something-or-other, had by now been isolated by Trevor Jackson and made into a formula that could be applied to pasture. In theory this mix is put underground, the grubs get crook, stop eating and die, and with enough remaining alive to infest the rest. So rather than wipe them out we needed to keep a few alive to keep the rest crook.

Getting the mixture — now called Invade, marketed by Monsanto — underground was to prove a new challenge.

Farmers and contractors Garry and Gay Hart allowed us to convert their Duncan seed drill and spray tank into a machine that would rip small furrows and inject Invade, closing the gaps again after it passed with a roller and harrows.

This product quickly made a difference. We were now only constrained by how much Invade we could afford, and how much ground we could graze out, drill and return to production. In total we drilled about 100 hectares.

Around this time another pathogen returned voluntarily. Bacillus papillae, something I'd never heard of. Our lawn was extensive, and so riddled with grass grubs that the lawnmower would roll up loose grass and choke in the worst parts.

The new visitor took them out comprehensively, over one season.

Rhone-Poulenc, a chemical company, were doing trials on the farm to determine the success of a product they were hoping to market to control grubs. It never worked well enough apparently but with extensive measuring and trialling over many months they discovered some astonishing figures. Where the pasture was dead to look at there were up to 3250 grass grubs per square metre.

Where the grass was merely sick-looking there were between 1500 and 2500 grubs per metre, and it was hard to find a population of fewer than 50 anywhere. Someone worked out that as few as 27 grubs per square metre had a deleterious effect on the quality of pasture.

During trips to the Wairarapa to buy rams we heard of, and then witnessed, heavy water-filled rollers being used to crush the grubs. Their shortcomings seemed to be that they dented, causing them to lose efficiency in ground contact. The purpose of rolling is twofold. It presses down the ruined grass 'mat' to help regrowth and it kills the grass grubs by squashing them.

In a book about pasture pests I found a double-ballasted roller that looked promising. Basically two rollers in tandem with a load between that could be as heavy or light as was necessary. Its drawback to me was price — around $12,000 at the time.

My attention was then drawn to road rollers. You know, the sort of thing you see at roadworks all around the country. Many of them are motorised and some are vibrating as well.

Those three-wheel monsters you see are also ballasted

with water so their weight can be increased or decreased as the need arises. For some time the idea of buying an old road roller really appealed, though again the disadvantages were to me too great. Too slow, too narrow, too old. Another factor was the tomo — underground holes unique to pumice country which have trapped many a tractor and bulk spreader. I could see myself with a massive 12-tonne roller lying on its side, cast in a tomo. A real threat. Every paddock we ploughed usually produced a couple close beneath the surface.

The process of slowly evolving pragmatism eventually produced an answer. A roller that was wide, fast and heavy enough to do real damage to grass grubs would be a large steel drum filled with concrete, towed by my existing wheel tractor, and would weigh in at around 10 tonnes.

I purchased an old diesel tank perfectly round, two metres high and three long. It doesn't pay to weld on old diesel tanks because of the risk of explosion, so I cut off its fittings with a disc grinder and cut two large holes in it, through which to pour concrete. Through the middle I put an old roller axle of around 50mm steel, and to each end of that I fitted a crude agricultural tyre bearing. From a neighbour an old Cambridge roller drawbar was gratefully accepted, modified and fitted to the bearings and axle so the whole thing was towable.

This large contraption was then backed up to the loading bank by the cattle yards with its opening facing upwards so we could make concrete and wheelbarrow it straight in. I arranged for a truckload of builder's mix and a truckload of river boulders and heaps of cement. The plan was to fill the tank with concrete, throw in boulders, cover with concrete and thus fill the tank to the top.

I should have got a tad suspicious when it took three of us eight hours working hard to fill it, with a large mixer that took a bag of cement at a time and around 65 shovels of metal.

Fill it we did, though. Then left it for some weeks to harden as we went about the business of regular farm work.

One day after completing a silage stack I was driving home past the roller with our number two tractor, a 55 HP Zetor. Thinking I would just hook up the roller and tow it home to weld up the openings. I carefully raised the drawbar, backed in, dropped in a drawbar pin and proceeded to drive home.

Except the roller would not move. At all. Intrigued, I uncoupled, drove home and got my larger, number one tractor, a 72 HP Ford 5000. I coupled this to the roller drawbar to transfer roller weight to the tractor's back wheels. This worked and I was away. Out from the cattle yards, 200 metres down the road and into the home section was the plan.

At this time the council were preparing our road for tar-sealing and had achieved a perfect surface just ready for the seal. As the road was slightly downhill, no sooner was I on the road than I thought I had better see if the beast behind the tractor would stop before I gathered too much speed. So I applied the brakes. The tractor stopped good as gold and I had a relieved grin. For a second. The tractor stopped all right, but the momentum of the roller bent its drawbar into a perfect arc and it came to rest hard on the tractor's back wheels.

Back to the drawing board. We put a tractor with a chain on each end of the roller, towed it off the road into the paddock in front of the house and shot back to carefully re-smooth the council's road. Then next trip to town I bought some serious steel and a gas welding set to cut it up with.

I measured and cut and welded and welded. In all my spare time, for ages. No great engineer am I. With the new drawbar lying on the shed floor carefully laid out, a tonne of steel was painstakingly put together.

Then came the time to take it all out of the shed, to turn it over so I could weld the other side. I welded an eye on the frame, lifted the whole thing out backwards with the front-end loader tied up with a chain. Just as the new piece reached optimum height to turn it over there was a mighty crack, the eye broke, the drawbar crashed down onto the front of the tractor. It smashed the tractor front cowling, and the radiator inside was as flat as a cowpat. Really wrecked. A fair bit of money later the tractor was repaired and drawbar turned, much more welding done and it was a very satisfying moment when I carried the drawbar to the roller on the front-end loader, very well and securely tied, and it fitted perfectly. Things were finally going to plan.

Bolted together, it was now three metres wide and five long. And looked formidable. Just to lift the drawbar to the tractor now took a decent jack arrangement, but I hooked up and was ready to go.

This time, to gather enough momentum to get the thing moving to cross the paddock, turn onto the road and turn down the drive, I rocked it backwards and forwards with the tractor until I was away. Then across the paddock in sixth gear, full revs, out onto the newly tarsealed road. But no, the second we were through the gate the ground rose slightly to the road level and the roller stopped dead. Two lovely matching holes in the new tarseal resulted. Some swearing now. More than a little pissed off, I gingerly backed off in such a way that I could turn 90 degrees and go through the drive gate and home. The drive gate and the roller were both three and a bit metres wide, so lining up the tractor seam with the gateway centre, I again took off. Alas, I was a hair's breadth out, the roller's side collided with the strainer post so hard it drove the stay right through the post and broke off the axle bearings. Completely blocking the driveway and necessitating another day's remedial action.

New bearing bolts, new strainer post and stay, and we were in action again, down the drive to the shed. Which was up a gentle incline, a metre or so higher than the surrounding section. Back and forwards I went, but no way was it going up there. So one day when the neighbours the Truebridges were going past with a much larger tractor they kindly towed the roller near enough to the shed to weld. And it was complete.

By now though I realised that my tractors were quite incapable of towing it anyway, so a major rethink was called for. And, to compound matters, we were made an offer on the farm too good to refuse and bought Retaruke station. A totally different class of country.

When the farm was on the market the agent politely commented that while there was no intention to disguise the grass grub problem, would it be possible to tow the roller away from the shed and park it somewhere less obtrusive?

Back to the Ford 5000, down the drive, into the paddock for four metres and dead stop. Right by the front gate. Six groups looked at the farm, four wanted to buy it, and no one asked what on earth the roller beside the front gate was for.

By now, even though the farm was sold, I just had to see if the damn thing worked. All through the grass grub experience AgResearch's Bruce Willoughby and others had been a lot of help and given heaps of advice, so I rang Bruce and suggested some before-and-after trials.

In other words, select a paddock, count the grubs, roll the paddock and count the grubs again. Sounds easy but it's a lot of work setting up grids, digging up hundreds of plots, counting grubs, and it has to be accurate.

We chose a flat paddock of three-year-old pasture that was infested and quite damaged by bull diggings. We borrowed Truebridges' gruntiest tractor — a Ford TW 20 with 150 horsepower on huge radial tyres for amazing traction — and away we went.

Just towing the roller was an experience. Across hard flat paddocks it was so heavy it created a small bow wave. It absolutely flattened everything in its path. Rabbit warrens were history, thistles looked as though they had been ironed, bull holes were levelled flat, and ridges left from previous winters disappeared.

Because of its width the roller behind this mighty tractor was able to cover two hectares an hour, even though at every corner all four wheels skidded as it turned. With such weight following behind the skidmarks were immediately pressed back flat so no damage resulted to the grass.

Bruce came back and recounted. Hours of work. The result fantastic. 50% killed in one pass, another 25% damaged so they would never eat again. Because of the compression factor another pass would have got them all. It worked; all the effort was worthwhile.

One question remained. What did it weigh? I have already noted that I am no engineer; neither am I a mathematician. So the AgResearch team did some calculations. Forty-three tonnes. Not bad for a 'ten-tonne' roller.

Up and Down the River

There's a huge amount of fun to be had in boats of all sizes, and I've enjoyed them all my life. We have had a jet boat ever since we moved to Retaruke in 1993. Living on a river means opportunity, but like all farmers we are usually too busy to go boating as often as we would like. We tend to go out more to show visitors around than for our own enjoyment.

The exception to this rule is rescuing people — compulsory boating no matter how much time is on hand. The Whanganui River experience attracts people of all levels of skill and adventure. Some, however, find themselves through their own inexperience, flood conditions or mechanical breakdown to be literally 'up the creek' without a paddle.

A classic situation to watch is where the husband, who has always driven the car and generally been in charge, is in the aft seat of a Canadian canoe with his much larger wife in the bow. Now, while both contribute to the paddling, most of the steering in a boat is done from the stern and a boat of any sort does not travel well with the bow down. So they tip out. Frequently. And what should be an enjoyable trip becomes frostier with every spill.

One very wet Easter a few years ago, Peter, Rachel and I were enjoying being inside after an action-packed sports day, when the Whakahoro hut warden came racing over. He had with him a canoeist from a large group who were in a spot of bother ten miles upstream.

We had trouble launching the boat, as the boat ramp was covered in mud from a receding flood and our digger wasn't anywhere near to clear the mud away. We launched anyway and motored upstream to a place near Tawata.

Two canoes that had been carrying four people had gone through the Tawata rapid and wrapped around a log. It was sticking out of the water by two metres or so and pointing upstream at about forty-five degrees. One of those feats that if you tried to do it, you couldn't. The wet ones had swum ashore, their gear rescued by the others in the group, and the whole lot were on the riverbank, a rocky ledge. Unbeknown to them, on the opposite side was a road within two hundred metres.

Peter managed to tie the bow of the first canoe to the jet boat cleat and we pulled it away from the log. Being plastic, it soon regained its normal shape, and after we had tipped the water out of it we towed it to the waiting canoeists.

The second canoe, the first to become entangled, was more than we could budge without wrecking it. After a few attempts at towing it away from the log we gave up to await the river dropping from its flood-high level. The pounding water was forcing the canoe onto and under the log. When the river dropped another two metres it would be high and dry.

We ferried the two brothers' canoes and their barrels of gear back to Retaruke, where they could await their friends who would arrive in a couple of hours. Then we spent a fair swag of time retrieving the jet boat. We finally had to use three vehicles coupled together to pull it through the mud and up the boat ramp. I don't like leaving the boat on the water when it's rising or falling from flood.

That was Easter. Six months went by and we never heard a word from anyone, so I sent the owner of the canoes an invoice for time spent rescuing his canoes. This was an uncharacteristic move from me, but I wasn't pleased. Peter and I had spent six hours, much fuel, a little risk, rescuing this clown's canoes. (A clown because he never should have put novice canoeists onto a rapidly rising river, and he had never said anything, not a phone call, not a card, not a thing. No thank you.) The response was a bit quicker this time. A terse letter to say he had taken legal advice and was under no obligation to pay anything, and I could get stuffed.

Years later, I think that I was only trying to make a point, the response which was ignorant and ill-considered. Nothing more was said or done, though I wished privately this particular canoeing operator would get in the shit and call for assistance as many do. But no such luck!

Along came Christmas and with it, Christmas cards, including three from grateful members of the tramping club we had rescued. The cards and the cheque the third card contained went a long way to restoring my faith in human nature.

***

Another memorable rescue happened when Robin from Wades Landing came over one evening. Rachel, Sam Rossiter and I were having a drink on the deck on a lovely summer evening. The warden from the John Coull Hut had radioed someone, who had rung Robin to say two of their canoeists were perched on a bank miles from anywhere, having lost their food, dry clothes, etc. Would we go?

The river was in pristine condition and within ten minutes Sam and I were off. Drinks left, boat fuelled, launched and evening darkness only an hour away, The only time to go was right away.

It was a smooth trip and sure enough the young women were sitting on a rocky bank, quite steep, huddled together and no doubt wishing they were anywhere else. We tied their canoe across the engine cover of our boat, gave them a coat each and were home within an hour of leaving.

The two girls were two of the most beautiful people I have ever seen. When they had left Retaruke to head down the river they had been nervous, out of their element. This had concerned Steve Carr of Wades Landing, but he was reassured by a group of Frenchmen who (naturally enough, in hindsight!) said they would keep an eye on the girls. They didn't. The girls lost their confidence after tipping out for the fourth or fifth time and just wanted to go home. They had showers at our place and warmed up with welcome hot drinks. Rachel fed us all and later when dinner was done, Sam took them to see the glow-worms between home and Lacys' bridge.

Sam said to me a few days later that if ever I needed a hand to rescue people from the river, I could rely on him. Steve fronted up with money for fuel, and life rocked on.

*

Three or four years ago Peter Lacy and I were working at the jet boat ramp on a Saturday morning. As the access to the boat ramp is on our land, Council or DoC do not maintain it, nor should they. We maintain it and on the day in question were loading the truck with river metal with our digger and spreading it on the boat ramp road. Peter was operating the digger and I was driving the truck. Just on lunchtime Mark Ebrey arrived with two buses with canoe trailers behind to pick up a number of canoeists who were part of an annual event, the Whanganui Descent. This race from Taumarunui to Retaruke has been held every spring since we have lived here and I'd forgot about it. Soon after Mark's arrival the first canoeists paddled in, led by the winner, Ben Fouhy.

Peter and I decided to get out of the way and go home for lunch. He shut off the digger, hopped in the truck and off we headed. Wet river metal is awfully heavy and the old truck was grunting with the effort. Being a New Zealand farmer I always overload things a bit. Around the corner from the boat ramp we met a vehicle head-on, driven by a man I shall call the Ugly American. A camouflage-painted ute, towing a camouflage-painted boat, driven by a couple wearing camouflage clothing.

The Ugly American leans out of his ute to tell me I should back up to let him through. I suggest I can't, as there are two buses and trailers behind me. He suggests I should, as he has to back a trailer and I don't, so I go backwards as far as I can. Not enough.

With evident bad grace and barely concealed mutterings the American backs away, we drive out and he drives in to launch his high-powered camouflaged boat.

I heard later that he considered the now full boat ramp and small beach a personal affront and called the assembling exhausted canoeists something to do with maternal incest. But he launched his boat, parked his ute and motored off. Still with bad grace, he set up such a wash as to sink the race's last two place-getters — probably the two most exhausted — and charged off down the river, noisy V8 and curses rippling in his wake. We knew none of this attitude until later, as Peter and I did a little more metalling and knocked off for the rest of the weekend.

The following day around two o'clock we had a ring from the lady where the American was staying.

"Is your jet boat going?" she asked.

Yes it was, I replied.

"Could you go down and see what's happened to our guest? He left yesterday for two hours' boating and hasn't come back." Twenty-six hours after he'd left; twenty-four hours overdue.

Now I have to admit a little reluctance, so Rachel and I had a bit of a yarn about whether we rescue only beautiful Danish girls or whether we rescue anybody who asks. Strangely I lost the debate. It doesn't pay to mention beautiful Danish girls too often.

I called my son Richie, who was keen, so we fuelled the boat and headed downstream. Forty minutes later, there was our American friend paddling his jet boat with one oar. Going with the river flow, days from the next boat ramp at Pipiriki and a day before Ramanui Lodge and the nearest help.

"Did you bring a battery?" were his first words. I couldn't contain myself and said "Yes, I always use a battery to start my motor." Without turning our engine off, we swung alongside and Richie quickly had our long heavy-duty jumper leads connected from our boat to theirs.

With a mighty roar their boat started and no sooner were the leads back aboard than he roared off up river, leaving us in his spray. Then he stopped again, his motor stalled. We pulled alongside and repeated the process. His battery, though near new, had no life and they had stopped to look for something. Off they roared again, much faster than us, and we didn't see them again until forty minutes later when we were driving our boat onto our trailer.

The American strode across to us as we secured our boat onto the trailer winch.

"Thanks a lot," he said, with a scowl that suggested his gratitude was not entirely genuine. "We didn't want to spend another two days drifting."

"No trouble," I said and tied up our bow rope. Richie pulled the boat forward and I walked behind to take out the bung to drain water from the hull.

"What do you drink?" asked the American.

"Don't worry about it," I replied, telling him we enjoyed the trip, but he wouldn't take that for an answer.

"What's your poison?" he asked again and again. After the third request, Richie volunteered that the old man could tolerate the odd drop of whisky.

"Whisky it is. One day soon you will come home, and watch out you don't trip up on a large bottle of whisky with a Black Label," said the American and he left to look after his boat.

We waved goodbye and drove home with mixed feelings, but knowing we had done the right thing. We're still waiting for that bottle, but. Maybe the American didn't realise prohibition still existed where he came from, or perhaps it got lost in the mail. It was just as well we weren't too thirsty. Or is it the thought that counts?

*

Sometimes when the rivers start to rise, the Retaruke, which flows into the Whanganui below our house, really rages. Usually later on the Whanganui rises and slows the Retaruke down, from what looks like over twenty knots to a mere crawl. During the raging stage the Retaruke is full of floating debris, and pressure waves are formed as the water forces its way through narrow reaches. It is quite frightening.

When canoeists reach the Retaruke they normally paddle a few hundred metres upstream to the boat ramp, from where it's another half-kilometre walk to the DoC hut where they often stay. There is no wet or dry season here. The lowest rainfall I've ever recorded was in midwinter and the wettest months have been in the spring and late summer.

One very wet August afternoon Rachel, our shepherd Nathan and I sat inside reading the weekend papers, which are delivered here on a Monday. Around two o'clock we looked out and noticed a group of a dozen people milling around in the pouring rain. They huddled together and didn't appear to have any direction. I asked Nathan to go out and see what was happening: who they were and what did they want? How come they were on our lawn?

Nathan took an umbrella and strode out, and was back in a couple of minutes, "They won't speak to me" he said, bemused.

"They'll bloody well talk to me," I said and strode out into the rain. Now, I'm no medical expert, quite the contrary, not bad with animals, with which I have had some practice. Hopeless with humans. Even to my untrained eye though, these people were utterly exhausted, suffering from shock, but mainly knackered. Summing up the situation as quickly as we could, Nathan and I grabbed an ATV and our biggest trailer. We loaded all their gear and hustled them around to the DoC hut. Not a word was spoken. We got a fire started in the hut and left them to it.

Later in the evening there was a knock on the door and the canoe group's organiser was there, all apologetic. They were twelve English doctors who had canoed down from Taumarunui the day before, had a bad night due to flooding at a campground upstream and had travelled here this morning. Wet and tired, they had tried for three hours to paddle up the Retaruke to safety. And they couldn't make it. Knowing no alternative they kept trying and trying, until beaten back by exhaustion and the raging Retaruke, when they discovered the track up to our place.

The bloke was really grateful for the help we had been able to offer and had brought over a bottle of port to say thanks. Not bad people, Pommy doctors.

*

I met Robert Muldoon twice when he was prime minister, and when I was very young and naive I was impressed with him. It was only years later when I got involved with farming politics that I discovered the tremendous damage he did to our economy. He put us back by more than a generation, trying to use devaluation to counter inflation. It cost us our trading advantage at a huge detriment to the country. I hope those Treasury officials who advised him got their beans, though I doubt they did.

I also remember Muldoon for some of the hard-case things be said. How New Zealanders immigrating to Australia raised the IQ of both countries. Even if he did borrow that from Tom Scott. His comments about a certain underarm bowling incident. His observation that New Zealand relying on tourism would make us into a nation of waiters.

This last remark hit the spot, as I've believed that for years and possibly always will. When we came to Retaruke we had no tourism aspirations, or any idea of the potential for tourism here. We were looking entirely at the prospects for the farm, always intent on being average or better farmers. Some time went by before we even realised the potential; cleaning the place up was the priority.

I've had to change my attitude somewhat as I came to realise visitors to the area know very little about stock management. It's up to me to have someone walk ahead of stock on public access and it's not up to me to ruin someone's holiday by swearing at their ignorance.

In the early days a man parked his car across a gateway that I was mustering heifers towards.

"Is my car in the way?" he asked.

"No," I replied, "Just open your other door and I'll drive the cattle straight through it."

I try to suppress such remarks these days.

One day Rachel and I left home at 7 a.m. to spend the morning doing stock work out on the farm. As often happens we spent much longer at it than we had planned and were actually heading home for lunch around 2 p.m. Coming through the bottom track paddock around a rocky and narrow bluff we came across a small mob of feral goats. I shot three, and when the bike was turned off while I processed them to take home for dog tucker, we heard two calves down in a gully. They had dropped off the track and down a steep slope about thirty metres. It took me another hour to catch them, hoist them out one at a time over my shoulders, and carry them back to the track where their mothers could find them. Then I gutted the goats and carried on home. Dirty, tired, thirsty and very hungry. Ambling around on the lawn by our house were two Germans. Tourists. A husband and wife couple with little English that I could understand.

They asked me where they could find 'Steve Canoe' — looking, I thought, to hire a canoe from Steve Carr at Wades Landing Outdoors. I washed my hands quickly, took off my boots, dialled Steve on the portable phone, gave the Germans the phone and went back inside to continue washing off the afternoon grime. When I came outside again the tourists were waiting for me, and said in German "Answer phone, no one home — what should we do?"

I took the phone back, looked up the number of another neighbour and rang them. Yes, they had a canoe available, so again I gave the phone over and left them to it. I had a glass of water, walked over to the toolshed, got out some dog tucker to defrost for tomorrow and put the goats I had brought home in the freezer.

When I returned they were still there. They wanted directions, so I pointed out where they should go to, and still they hung around. Next they wanted to know the difference in price to hire canoes from Steve Canoe and the other neighbour, and finally I got a bit grumpy. These people were rude, ignorant and hard to please; I obviously wasn't a canoe operator, was only trying to be helpful. "Look," I said, by this time thinking of them as Adolf and Eva, "You've flown out here from Germany, first class for all I know, you've hired a brand new car and driven here from Auckland, and here you are moaning to me about who charges what for whatever. Bugger off!"

My voice was quiet but clear: "Get out of here, go on get off the place."

They looked at me aghast, turned and left.

Canoe operator number two rang me a week later to thank me for sending them over. He'd given them dinner, bed and breakfast, hired them a canoe and collected them at the end of their trip for another dinner, bed and breakfast. Charged them the best part of a thousand dollars. He said they were polite and very quiet, but thought I was a bit of a rough character. Any time I wanted to break in tourists and send them over was fine by him.

*

Jet boating by its very nature is a fairly high-risk sport. The jet unit itself, invented by South Island sheep farmer Bill Hamilton, enables the boat to go through very shallow water, and in our case around some rather large rocks and logs.

Often a moment spent on our bridge — from where you can plan a route through the water from the boat ramp, through a few rocks, one narrow rapid, and a rock shelf and around some fallen trees — is time well spent.

I've seen experienced 'expert' boaties hit them all, some so hard their boats have leapt out of the water. The river also changes a little all the time. Being observant and reading the water are vital, as is good maintenance, plus a little caution.

On Dan's twenty-first birthday a few jet boat trips were in order for the guests, so we launched the boat first thing on the day of the party and set off, telling Rachel we'd only be gone thirty minutes. It was a tidy fibreglass boat, well maintained by its previous owner and ourselves. About six minutes down river were a small series of rapids and rocks, a left-hand curve, one hundred metres straight, then a sharp right, quick left and right again and a touch left. No trouble; I'd been through half a dozen times in the past couple of months. Except when it came to the last touch left there was no steering and we crashed hard into a solid rock standing three metres out of the water. At around forty kilometres an hour. (This series of obstacles has changed many times since then, with the present boating course going thirty metres away from it.)

We stuck, hard. The 16-foot boat hit on the starboard side a metre from the bow, which was split from the topside deck to midships, with eight ragged rips in the hull from top to bottom. It was sinking quite quickly, and my starboard leg was jammed between the floor and underneath the dashboard.

I yelled to nephew Jamie to paddle to the left bank, which he started to immediately. The current helped us go in that direction.

"We're sinking," he shouted.

"I know," I replied. "Paddle faster!"

Then the boat sank in shallow water on the left bank. I extricated my quite stiff and sore leg and the five of us scrambled through the shallows to shore. The most fortunate, maybe the only fortunate, thing was that no one other than me was hurt, and me not badly. No one was very happy of course, but we were intact.

We tied the boat to a tree and spent the next few minutes discussing what to do. I recommended that we should stay together rather than one of us head for home, and we headed upriver in a group, walking along a soft wet grassy bank. We were only a few kilometres from home, but proceeding quite slowly as one of our party was having difficulty keeping up. The going was good for the first kilometre or so and as we only had five to go, we were quite optimistic. But while boating the river and concentrating on the water I had never studied its banks too closely, and we soon came to an impassable rock face.

We backtracked until we found a way inland, up a steep creek bed and into the surrounding native bush, National Park proper. Full of pig rooting, making the ground rough as guts, and supplejack, making the ground even more difficult to pass over. I have never seen so much supplejack. Tina was going slowly and after a while I decided to comment on this. She replied that it was her jeans slowing her down. Out with my ever-present Swiss army knife and her jeans quickly became shorts, but her walking didn't speed up at all. Away from the river we climbed onwards and upwards to go around the riverside bluffs. This is a steep, remote wilderness where only very experienced hunters usually go. After two hours or so of this we reached a ridge and sat down for a break and to assess our situation. We could actually see the holding paddocks within 200 metres of home, though for us they were many hours away. Then across the river I heard a dog barking and remembered that Rakau Nikora was staying at Whitianga Marae for the weekend.

I stood and shouted out *"Rakau!"* as loud as only a hill

country musterer can, twice. We waited and waited for what seemed like five minutes, but was probably only one.

A child's voice, one of Rakau's children, called back. "Who's that?"

As loud as I could I shouted back, "It's Richard, get Rakau."

We waited and waited. Then Rakau's voice. "Who's there?"

"It's Richard. Call Rachel. Get help!"

We waited and waited some more.

"Who's Rachel?" Rakau replied.

This was painful. "Rachel Steele! Call her, get help, boat's sunk."

This all seemed to take ages; we were a long way apart and couldn't see each other. After a while Rakau had it sorted. Unknown to us, the shipwrecked, he took his boat over to our place and told Rachel someone was yelling at him from somewhere in the bush about their boat being sunk.

Rachel had known we were late and that something was wrong, and had already rung the Department of Conservation for help. They told her that they always wait six hours, in case the overdue group turn up of their own volition. She then rang our neighbours, the Ruslings — who have two jet boats — but their two drivers were away on a first aid course so they could use their boats commercially. They couldn't be contacted.

Unaware of these difficulties and confident that help was on the way, we trudged back down to the river and waited on the bank. Eventually Steve Dempsey arrived to rescue us. It took a while, because when he was contacted the timing gears were out of his motor and he had to put it back together before he could set off.

It was a huge relief to be back at home, eight hours after we had left for half an hour.

The party continued most successfully, as parties stacked with Massey university students are wont to do. Ivan Rusling took a few people down the river the next day to assess the damage. They unbolted the motor so it could be taken home. Which it was on the following Monday, the motor in one load and the hull in another. Sitting in the school paddock, it was a sorry sight.

A lot of lessons were learnt:

— I'd thought the maintenance on the boat was up to scratch, but something in the steering failed: exactly what, we have never determined.
— There is no harm doing more checking.
— When someone is overdue, go looking straight away. Better a wasted trip than to arrive at an accident scene too late.
— Carry enough gear to be able at least to light a fire. Being on the riverbank warm has to be better than sitting and freezing.

Lots of people gave other well intended advice, but it's likely that if you go jet boating on any river, an accident is going to occur sometime. As we say on the farm, if you've never lost a truckload of hay, you probably haven't carted much. All the gear from the wrecked hull went into a new aluminium hull we bought, and like Grandfather's old axe — the one that has had three new heads and four new handles but "it's still the same old axe" — a new boat continued its adventures.

*